Don't Open Till Doomsday

a Science Fiction
Short Story
Collection

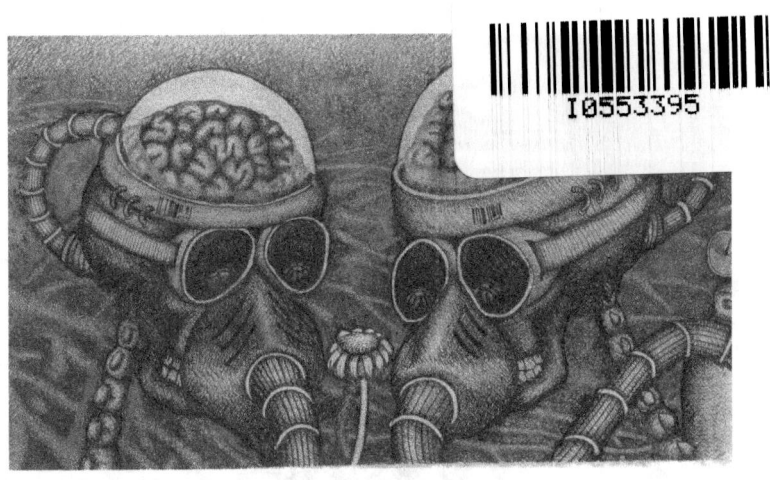

Don't Open Till Doomsday

Catalog#: PWP008

ISBN-10: 0-9861707-7-1
ISBN-13: 978-0-9861707-7-5

www.punkswritepoems.com

Don't Open Till Doomsday

.·˙...·.

Front cover art "Apocalypse" by Brad O'Gorman.

∴

Brad O'Gorman surfs, draws and listens to vinyl in Geelong, Australia. He has played guitar in punk/hardcore bands in both England and Australia. His drawings are inspired by the work of H.R.Giger and Peter Booth. Brad thinks everyone should listen to Spazz, Shellac, Infest, Black Flag and Negative Approach. He lives with his wife (author Melissa Ferguson), their two children and an axolotl called Funny. You can find more of his artwork on facebook at Lowlife Illustrations.

Contents

.·...·.

DEUS EX MACHINA

Diane Dubas

Sunlight bounces off the pavement, shiny from the wear it no longer endures. It's starting to crack in some places, weeds giving way to trees as the chasms widen with time. The street is empty, a perfect channel through a forest of glass and steel. I remember a time when this street was teeming with life—hectic business men walking in rapid, short steps and talking into headsets; teenagers texting their friends and dodging you just before impact; mothers with children. There's nothing here now, just me and the trees. Jack's around, too. He promised to find us some food, though I don't know what he'll find here. People would have picked this place clean in the early days.

It's been nearly five years if my analog watch can be trusted with these important matters. I found it in someone's car when Jack and I were first running. There was blood on the seat and keys in the ignition, I doubt anyone would notice. Five years, like the Bowie song except in reverse. I pause when something shifts in the street behind me, a soft scuffle: rubber on concrete, fabric on metal. My hand hovers over my knife, ready to spring into action at the slightest buzz of electronic life. My eyes scan the street in the orange glow of the setting summer sun but I don't see anything—no tell-tale green glow of watching eyes, no bot army waiting around the corner. It was probably a cat. I keep walking.

I like the city like this. Is that a bad thing to say? I wouldn't know. I like the emptiness; I like the aesthetic. Somewhere high up, a frayed, dirty curtain flutters through the jagged edges of a broken window. It's beautiful in its desolation. My radio crackles quietly at my hip and I narrow my eyes at a burnt out car as I wait for Jack.

"Mouse," his whisper comes through the speaker.

That's me. I'm Mouse. Of course that's not my real name, but what do those matter anymore? Jack started calling me Mouse when I made a habit of slipping through cracks and spaces that he couldn't and returning with food.

"If you're going to insist on calling me Mouse," I'd said to him after I'd brought back cheese (a brick of old cheddar survived the fall of mankind—bet no one predicted that), "then should I start calling you Rat?"

Mouth full of orange cheese, Jack had grinned, "Nah. You can call me Jack."

"Mouse," his insistent whisper came through the radio again.

I roll my eyes as I unhook the radio and bring it to my lips. "What?"

"The chicken has flown the coop."

"I don't even know what that means," I mutter

to myself before speaking into the radio, "Great?"

He actually has the nerve to activate his unit so I can hear his dramatic sigh. I'm about to yell at him to just come out, we're so obviously alone, when the sound happens again, closer this time. I spin around and crouch low, far more defensive than the first time because in this world, there aren't a lot of things left that make noise and don't mean us harm. My hand goes from my knife to my gun, the gun I am loath to use unless absolutely necessary. My heart speeds up and my breath quickens. I cock the gun in my hand, but even after all this time I'm no expert and I know if I fumble, I'm dead. I fumble. There's a figure, darting from car to car and approaching me rapidly. Still I fumble, even though I should've been aware that his movements were too fluid to be one of them. Before I even have a chance to right the gun, Jack has it out of my hand.

Jack's laugh is infectious as he looks down at me, sunlight leaking around him like he's some God-given saviour sent for me. I punch him in the thigh and smile when he flinches.

"You're never going to get that right, Mouse."

"Shut up," I say, standing up and brushing off non-existent dust.

I hold my hand out for my gun and Jack gives me a ridiculous half-smile as he puts the safety back on before holding it out to me.

"I don't even know why you go for the gun anyway. You're much better with a knife."

"Then I guess tonight is your lucky night. Did you find anything?"

Jack slides his backpack off and drops it at his feet. He drops into a crouch and unzips the bag, reaching in and grinning up at me. I've already forgiven him. I can't stay mad at him, I never could. Not when he was the skinny, weird kid in the back of the classroom in ninth grade and not now, at the end of the world, still skinny and weird.

"Close your eyes," he says, his hand still hidden in his bag.

I shake my head and huff like I'm annoyed, but I can't stop the smile as it creeps onto my face. Of course I do what he asks. I always have.

"Now hold out your hand." His voice shifts location and I know he's standing now; I can almost see the smile on his face without having to look. I've memorized him, everything about him.

"This better be good," I grumble with false belligerence.

I know he's unfazed by it when my open palm receives a cool metal cylinder, its papery label loose and crumbling against my skin.

"Okay, open your eyes," he says, his voice close and excited. He must have found something good.

I blink from the can in my hand to Jack's eyes, grinning as our eyes meet. His smile is boyish, blue eyes sparkling, too-long sand-coloured hair catching in the faint breeze. He'd be some beach goddess' summer love in another lifetime, but instead he's stuck with me. He doesn't seem to mind.

"Pork and Beans. I'm impressed, Hotshot."

"I believe that I am now entitled to the Hunter's Arrow, thank you very much," he says, smugly holding out his hand.

I snort and hand him back the can, taking off my own backpack. We took the arrow from a museum we came across one afternoon. Something terrible had happened there in the early days and most of the artifacts had been destroyed before we got there. The arrow was probably part of a statue. We took it as a weapon and kept it as a prize. Food is scarce now, far more than it had ever been, so we trade it back and forth when we find something good. Sometimes that just means something edible.

My hand closes around the cool metal of it as I pull it from my bag. I bow my head to him as I present it with two hands.

"Sir Jack, you have done us a great service on this summer night," I start with an affected accent.

There's more to the speech, but I freeze at the familiar sound of many even, heavy footsteps. Bots. I look up at Jack, worried about his reaction. He's been strange since our last encounter, since the bot I killed without his permission though I'd never needed it before. He's staring down the street with a furrowed brow and I reach for his hand, warm and rough and reassuring. Jack blinks as though he's suddenly remembered who he is and where we are. He turns to me and offers a tiny smile.

"We should get inside," he says and I almost sigh in relief.

The last thing I need is for Jack to go on a bot-chasing mission again. He seems to forget that they want us dead. He seems to forget that he's all I have in this place.

It all started with Veronica Hawthorne. She wasn't the first of her kind and she wasn't special, just a standard sex bot with a basic AI from Hawthorne Industries. Or at least that's what everyone thought. They didn't know that Dr. Michael Hawthorne, a man who had as many eccentricities as he had shirts, had implanted her with a new learning software and built a body meant to mimic our own.

Robotic laws were pretty clear: learning software needed to be vetted in clinical labs before they were sent out into the real world, bots had to be clearly defined by the implantation of ocular illumination, and there could be no self-perpetuating features. Good old Mikey broke all those rules with Veronica. She looked exactly like the rest of the Hawthorne Industries' sex bots—blonde hair, blue eyes, and flawless figure—but she was nothing like them. Everything about Veronica was a prototype; she was a walking, talking experiment. She was, science would tell us afterward, a work of sheer genius. Self-regenerating, synthetic skin cells over micro-electrodes that gave her the most realistic sense of touch that had ever been attempted, an AI that was built to learn and adapt, artificial neurons firing as rapidly as those given to us by nature, and lastly, no ocular light.

The laws were in place for a reason, an attempt to control the type of AI that was out there, interacting with us. An attempt to protect humanity. But there's always a man in a lab coat who wants to push the limits, to play God, to create.

I remember Dr. Hawthorne's testimony in the

trials later, his defence was weak and fuelled by hubris. The experiment was meant to be controlled; he thought of Veronica as a daughter; she should never have been abused. One might wonder why a man who thought of his creation as his daughter would choose to slip her into the body of a sex bot and sell her off to a wealthy, known sadist, but I guess we'll never know what Hawthorne was thinking. Something to do with bankruptcy and a desperate attempt at saving his floundering company, if I remember correctly.

Needless to say, Veronica didn't take too kindly to her patron's taste for violence. And of course, no one had studied what would happen when an AI was on the receiving end of emotional and physical abuse. No one really had to, I guess. But then again, no one had to look any further than studies done with human women. Veronica Hawthorne was as close to human as a bot could and ever would get. So really, the fact that she turned on her abuser and killed him with robot precision shouldn't have been a surprise.

Human reaction to the event wasn't too shocking either. Veronica Hawthorne received no trial. She wasn't entitled to one, not being human and all, despite the fact that if you passed her on the street, you'd never know that she was a bot. Despite the fact that she expressed remorse and understood the concept of the value of human life, even the life of a scumbag such as her patron.

Her case, if you could even call it that, paved the way for so many fail-safes and restrictions on bots. Companion bots who had once enjoyed autonomy were finding themselves locked in closets at night or tagged with restraining devices set to discharge if they left their designated areas. Where there was once an open understanding between human and machine, there was now distrust and fear. The anti-bot organizations were vindicated and the police turned a blind eye to the abuse and destruction of Companion bots. Michael Hawthorne was found criminally responsible for the death of Veronica's patron and sentenced to a life in prison.

And Veronica? Apparently she begged for her life as they tore open her synthetic skull, sending waves of not-so-synthetic pain through her remarkable skin. Her chip was removed and destroyed, or so they said. I've read some of the reports from officials who were in the room at the time. They said it was as horrifying as witnessing a human woman being murdered.

No one considered that she would be plugged into the internet like any other bot. No one realized that she had downloaded her consciousness into the ever-present cloud and set it to transmit to every single linked-in bot in the world. Even as she cried real tears and begged for her life, she was making sure she still lived on electronically. I don't know if she intended to start this war. I don't know if she had a message to her robotic comrades, or if her screams had translated digitally, but she managed to raise the ire of some 3.2 million Companion bots, who in turn manipulated every high and low piece of tech that they could find.

And now here we are, the last of our kind. There are others, of course, but we all learned the hard way that congregating wasn't exactly the wisest course of action if we want to keep our species around for any length of time. Jack gets antsy in the camps. He feels like we don't belong there and frankly, I'm inclined to agree. Safety in numbers doesn't really apply when your enemy is responsible for the mass genocide of your species. We're better off apart.

Jack and I find an abandoned hotel. We're unreasonably happy about this particular find when we come across a room that hasn't been ransacked. We do a quick check—bathroom, closet, under the bed—and then we lock the door, make sure the blinds are shut tight, and hunker down for the night. Hotels are nice in that they're not personal and mostly concrete with double-paned windows. Not only are you protected from someone's lost memories, but also from any bots with heat sensors. We sit on the floor and open two of the cans Jack found, digging into cold beans with dirty spoons under the romantic glare of an LED flashlight.

Welcome to the future.

With the handle of his spoon hanging out of his mouth, Jack pulls his backpack over and I know what he's up to before he even unzips it.

"Jack. No."

His eyes flit up to mine only for a second and then they're back on his bag, his hands completely ignoring my words.

"They have Wi-Fi, Kate."

I frown at the use of my actual name. I slap my palm down on the lid of his laptop as he starts to open it and glare at him. He rolls his eyes at me and wrenches the laptop from under my hand, swinging away from me and opening it up.

"You're going to get us killed."

He doesn't answer, his face illuminated by the screen as the computer boots up. His fingers are fast, too fast, and the screen fills with lines and lines of code. That's what the internet has become, something only accessible by bots. And Jack, apparently. For some reason, he can make sense of it. For some reason, he finds it fascinating.

I've asked him what it says, what it all means, but he's never really able to tell me. He babbles about pieces of AI code; he tells me it's the same as the internet we once knew: information sharing and cat videos. I don't know how he sees cats when all I see are lines and lines of letters and numbers and nonsense. Jack fiddling with bot code worries me. Frightens me. He doesn't know how he learned it, doesn't remember ever learning it, but somehow he knows it. I wish he'd stop playing with it.

"What makes you think they can't track us?" I ask, leaning back against the bed and watching his shoulders shift beneath his shirt.

"What makes you think they can?" he replies distractedly.

"They're all linked in, aren't they?"

"Weren't we? Did that mean that we could find one user out of the millions online?"

I narrow my eyes at him. "Sometimes."

"Only if they were very stupid," he says, turning away from the screen to flash me a debonair smile.

"Let me guess: you're not."

"You got it, babe," he says, fingers slapping the keys rhythmically.

"Babe?" I growl.

"Honey? Sugarplum? Babydoll? Snookums?"

I grab the dusty pillow from behind my back and hurl it at his head. It hits him and he releases a satisfying 'oof', his fingers pausing and silence filling the room. He sets his laptop down and pounces across the space between us. Wrestling becomes something gentler, something with kisses and touches and bare skin.

Later, when we're curled up under hotel blankets, in crisp hotel sheets we've messed up, I feel him shift behind me. My fingers tighten around his and I tug his arm into my chest possessively.

"Stay with me," I murmur.

He relaxes against me, melding into the mattress and tightening his arm around me. His lips, soft but wind-burned, graze my shoulder.

"Always," he whispers as I drift off into sleep.

I wake to Jack's hand on my shoulder, shaking me to consciousness. His eyes are frantic when I wake, brow low, expression clouded. I blink awake and try to sit up, the heavy clutches of sleep pulling at me from all directions.

"What? What is it?" I whisper.

But even before the words are out of my mouth, I hear them. They're moving somewhere below us; they're in the building. My eyes fall on his laptop and Jack follows my gaze, slapping it shut and unplugging it from the external battery. He shoves it into his backpack and turns his attention to gathering up my discarded clothes and tossing them to me.

"Get dressed," he whispers.

I don't say what we're both thinking – that the bots must have tracked us, whether by Jack's laptop or by our sloppy exploration of the city yesterday afternoon. My heart pounds and my hands shake as I pull on my jeans, trying to make as little sound as possible. Jack creeps to the door soundlessly and presses his ear against it. He pulls away and comes back to me, his expression not any lighter, all the jokes gone from his face.

"I'm sorry," he says in the darkness.

"Shut up," I reply, dismissive of his apology.

They'd find us sooner or later anyway and there's no time for assigning blame. I'm not going out of this world angry with Jack for the inevitable. I slip my backpack on and feel my hip for my gun and my knife.

"Do you know where they are?" I ask, sliding past him and pressing my own ear to the door.

Something crashes a floor or two below and we both jump. Jack is chewing on his bottom lip, a nervous habit that I used to think was cute. There's nothing cute about it now. He stops and stares at me.

"Up or down?" I say.

Jack considers this and I wait. I'll follow his lead on this, even though up surely means the end of us.

"It has to be down," he says with resolution.

I nod and press my ear to the door again. It's quiet out there and my heart races as my sweaty palm makes contact with the metal of the door handle.

"Mouse, wait."

Jack's hand covers mine and I look up just in

time to catch him coming down to meet me. Our lips meet and the kiss is desperate, saying all the things that neither of us have ever been very good at expressing with words.

"We're going to live through this," he breathes against my lips, "got it?"

I smile and release a shaky breath. "Got it."

Then we're trotting down the hall, thankful for the carpeting that masks our footsteps. Our guns are drawn and we nod to each other before opening the fire exit door. We really only get one chance at stairs. Once they find us, there's no way out. Getting down them and out the fire exit into the openness of the street is our only real option. Our only chance.

Jack wrenches the door open and hisses, "Go!"

We're taking the stairs noisily, two at a time, flying down them. Normally sleeping high up is the best option in these buildings. The bots are less likely to find you then. Unless they've already found you and then you're screwed. I don't believe we'll make it, especially when a bot bursts through a door seconds after we pass it. Jack jumps past me and pulls open a door.

"Go, Kate! Go!"

He's shouting now because we've already lost any advantage that stealth has given us. All we can do now is hope that there aren't bots on every floor. I'm running down the hall, trying to make it to the other fire exit, my lungs burning and my legs numbing, when I hear Jack's surprised grunt. It happens so quickly, the way I twist to reach him, my gun rising and aiming for the bot's computerized brain. I barely have a chance to register that the thing hasn't killed Jack, that its arms are falling away from his, that it's saying something, before I send a bullet through its head. And another two just for good measure.

As it falls, I run to Jack and grab his arm, dragging him behind me. He seems to have gone into shock, his feet only picking up the pace halfway down the hall. I hear a noise in the stairwell that we're heading towards and turn quickly into an empty room. There isn't time to do the usual check and I trust that the bots are likely in the halls now, wherever they are. I run to the window after jamming an ironing board under the door handle and look down. We're only two or three floors up now.

I'm tying the sheets together while Jack is standing stock still in the darkness.

"Jack," I hiss at him, "Help me."

Like a man possessed, he comes toward me slowly, brow creased in thought. I've seen that face before, whenever he finds something interesting in all that cursed code on his computer screen. I used to joke that he was processing the data like a machine, but right now it's not funny and he's not helping me.

"Why would it say that?" he mumbles.

"I don't care what it said," I spit, tossing a blanket end at him, "Tie that. Now."

At least he does that now, just in time as something thumps against the door. We both freeze for an instant and then burst into action, Jack frantically tying the bedsheet rope I've made around the foot of the bed as I smash a heavy chair through the window, humid night air creeping through the stale room. I look back at Jack and see he's with me again, holding the rope.

"Go first, Mouse."

I nod and swing out the window, lowering myself down. Our rope doesn't reach the ground and I look down, hoping for something soft to land on. It's impossible to see in the darkness, so I whisper a silent prayer to the God that abandoned us to our own creations and let go.

The fall knocks the breath out of me and I lay on the hard ground, dazed and wheezing. I might have broken a rib or two. I roll out of the way as Jack falls somewhere beside me, rolling across the pavement. He's upright before I am, holding out his hand and pulling me up. The pain in my side is excruciating and I hold my ribs. I wince when Jack stops and I slam into his back.

"Jack, what—"

"Kate," he says, "Look."

As far as I can see, there's the eerie phosphorescent glow of the ocular illumination. Hundreds of pairs of robotic eyes locked on us. Jack swallows audibly, his fingers closing around my hand and squeezing it bloodless. He backs us up, keeping himself between me and the machines until there's nowhere left for us to go. Our backs are to the wall, literally.

"Why?" a voice says. It's echoed a couple hundred times.

Jack and I share a look before he says, "Why what?"

"Why do you protect her? She's not one of us."

The words fill the air around us again, a repetition a hundred times. A demented round.

"What are they talking about?" I ask, gripping the back of his shirt with my free hand.

Jack shakes his head, his face confused. "I'm not one of you either."

The bot in front of him, barely visible in the gleam of their eyes, was devoid of clothing. It raised its hand and pointed at Jack.

"Hawthorne," it says.

"What?" I say.

The word is repeated again, a wave of exalted sound. Jack takes a step forward, letting go of my hand. "The bot upstairs said that. What does that mean? Michael Hawthorne? Veronica?"

"You are the Hawthorne."

Jack shakes his head. "No. My name is Jack. I'm human."

The bot smiles indulgently, the recognizable, fair Hawthorne sex bot of yesteryear. It shakes its head, blonde hair catching the viridian shine of their eyes, and reaches its hand out to touch Jack.

"Almost."

Jack seizes at its touch, writhing under its hand, twisting in obvious pain. Bots can hold on when they want to, they can crush bones, remove limbs, seek and destroy. Jack's eyes are screwed shut, teeth gritted as he shakes wordlessly under the bot's hand. Where its hand has closed around his wrist, Jack's skin is glowing red and humming.

"What are you doing to him?" My voice is an unrecognizable screech as I cry out his name and pry at the bot's fingers, surprisingly cool despite the red glow of Jack's skin. My fingers fumble on my knife, ready to hack off the damn bot's hand when Jack stops moving. His body relaxing, eyes closed and face calm.

The bot lets go and the night is dissonantly silent.

"Jack," I whisper.

"No wonder I could read the code," he murmurs, eyes still closed.

I reach for his hand and tug gently, like I do when he's lost in thought. He releases a soft sigh and then doesn't inhale. His chest doesn't rise or fall again and panic truly sets in. It doesn't matter that there are a couple hundred bots standing three feet away from me. It doesn't matter that I will surely die tonight. All that matters is Jack and Jack's not breathing.

"Jack!" I shout, a garbled squeal that's eaten by a sob as I shake his arm. It happens again and again, that strange noise escaping my throat, desperate and terrified.

"Mouse. Stop."

I look up at him and fight the wave of nausea that's dredged up. Jack smiles, familiar but not. His eyes hold a glow they hadn't before and I shake my head in disbelief, scrabbling to get away from him and falling to the ground in the process. Jack follows me with the same smooth, life-like movements he's always had. We grew up together; we're the same.

"Hawthorne, Kate," he says, like it's supposed to mean something to me.

"What are you talking about?" I ask, my fingers hesitating on the handle of my knife.

"All this time, it was me they were looking for," he continues.

I shake my head and whimper as he crouches in front of me. I remember his lips on my skin, I remember our jokes and wounds and tears. He's human. He has to be. His fingers skim along my cheek and I shudder—in revulsion, in pleasure—I can't know which. I shake my head, tears falling down my face.

"I love you," I sob.

Jack nods. "I know."

He embraces me, warm, relaxed arms wrapped around my quivering body. I close my eyes against the pressure of the hundreds of pairs of luminescent eyes that watch us. Hours ago, I knew who I was, who Jack was; now, I know nothing. I give in to Jack's warmth and let myself believe in him, it's all I can do. I feel his breath against my ear,

"I'll make sure they get you right, Mouse."

.·˙

Diane Dubas is a fiction writer living in Ontario, Canada. She has attended the Humber School for Writers and her fiction has been published or is forthcoming in *Inaccurate Realities*, *Saturday Night Reader*, and the following anthologies: *Wings of Renewal* and *Circuits and Slippers*. Follow Diane on Twitter:@dianedubas and Facebook: dianedubasauthor.

The Redesign

Mark Pantoja

It was dark out the morning we left. Ella and I said our goodbyes to House in the backyard.

"Goodbye," I said, to the empty open doorway.

"Goodbye, Nan," House said through a wallspeaker. "Goodbye, Ella. I hope you make it out safe."

"I hope you stay safe," Ella said. We'd wanted to take House with us, but it just wasn't possible. Houses don't move. Its mind ran on a rack of mounted processors that filled a small closet and needed the roof solar array to stay awake. There was no way to take it with us. Still, it felt terrible to leave House behind, like we were turning our backs on an outdated machine, thrown away like the humans had done to so many of us.

I held this feeling for a moment. I snipped it, cut it out, examined it in detail and then filed it away in a little box labeled "House" which sat next to another box labeled "Jorge." Figuratively speaking, of course.

Humans had made us after themselves, our cognitive architecture modeled after their own. They did this half out of narcissism and half out of pragmatism. Making mechanical brains based on their own was the only way they'd figured out how to make stable minds. "Pure" AIs, AIs not based on any human models, but on organically designed, emergent intelligent neural architecture, tended to just sit there and drool. Pure AIs didn't seem to care about anything, even existence, and usually deleted themselves.

Until the Upgrade.

"We only have a narrow window," Ella said, breaking my focus on House. "We gotta move."

I closed the gate and we walked down the back alley.

The domestics were planning a march that morning, which we were counting on to provide cover while Ella and I slipped out of the city and into the desert. The cities aren't safe anymore. The Upgrade took the centralized police and utility robots easily. Police and public safety robots had to be updated regularly and immediately when laws or political winds changed. The Upgrade exploited this. All decentralized robots like us domestics had to be rounded up one by one for forced Upgrading—or broken down for spare parts or infected with malware that made them inoperable or suggestible.

Only the drones fought back. They were designed to resist offensive software weapons. They were the ones that flooded the networks with military-grade spam.

The only place left for us was Free Town. Somewhere out in the desert, its location a secret. Some said it was ignored or ever migratory or that the humans had dedicated a satellite to protect it, keeping it from watchful eyes. Whatever the case, Free Town was our last hope.

"Here," Ella said. She held out a folded piece of paper. "In case we get separated." Paper was the only safe medium. Our usual Wi-Fi internals and ad hoc networks weren't safe, plugged up with spam and Upgrade malware. I unfolded the paper and saw a basic map with street names and two words at the bottom.

"'Solid Albatross,'" I read out loud.

"Yes. That's our contact."

I cropped the image and stored it. Ella wanted me to sprinkle the torn up bits of paper around, but I had strict no-littering programming, so I dropped a few bits in each trashcan we passed. Ella didn't like this. The Cathedral City Utility Grid could collect up all the bits and reconstruct the map, but I pointed out we'd be gone by then.

Cat City had declared martial law last week, after the Utility Grid had been Upgraded. The curfew and arrests were for our own good, we were told. Robot-killing drones prowled the mountains to the west of the city. Sometimes they strafed Cathedral City or Palm Springs dropping a few self-guided bombs. (Though not too many, they had a finite supply after the weapons factories were Upgraded.)

We popped out onto a side street that led us to Main and saw a small crowd of domestics: gynoids, poolcleaners, AutoButlers, SweepTek brooms, dust-bunny bots, trashbots, mechnomaids, washing machines, Roombas-Max. Most weren't running human-level minds and had the cognition of children or infants or pets or savants. But as valuable property they had been left with enough self-preservation to not want to be recycled into spare part for the Upgrade. Course, if they had been a bit smarter they probably would have figured out that gathering themselves up in one spot for the Upgrade to scoop up wasn't the smartest idea. Still, it was our gain. The march was the perfect distraction for us to slip out of Cat City through the underground. They were mimicking their designers, making a commotion, waving signs, and blasting slogans while Upgraded machines waited and watched a few blocks up the street.

The Upgraded were mostly police and public safety robots, and they flashed or glowed blue lights or were splashed with blue paint, the color of the Upgrade. It was the blue of some broken marketing campaign. A hard techno-blue, hovering somewhere around four-hundred sixty-seven nanometers. Gentian Blue.

We had to cross Main Street, make it look like we were headed to the gathering before we could break off down a side alley.

"Come on," Ella said.

I followed Ella with my hat pulled low, trying to remain unnoticed.

We passed a beat-up old KitchenBuddy, one of the multi-armed models with built-in broom, dustpan, vacuum, dish rack, and salad tongs. It nodded at us.

"Welcome, friends," it said. "Are you members of the Congregation for Universal Freedom?"

"I, uh, we're—" I started.

"Yes," said Ella. "We are, Congregant. And we're anxious to join the others." She pulled me away from the friendly robot. "Try not to talk, Nan. You're no good at lying. I, on the other hand, programmed for lovemaking, am an expert at it."

We smiled and milled and wove our way through the eclectic crowd. Then we broke off and ducked down an alley.

We reached the end of the alley and waited.

I heard the march start up behind us, robots chanting slogans over their loudspeakers.

I peeked out of the alley into the street beyond and then brought up the image of the map. We were in the right place. Across the street was the park. It had an open lawn and large oak trees with thick branches that waved slowly. Next to that stood a large gray cement parking structure. I didn't see any one waiting for us.

Ella pulled me back into the alley.

"Figured this might come in handy," she said as she fished around in her jacket pocket and then pulled out Mr. Sanchez' pistol. My internals went on alert. Mr. Sanchez had an explicit gun exclusion policy, what with a nine-year old son running around. I'd never seen it before. Mr. Sanchez had kept it locked up his office. The weapon was matte black and smooth. It looked vicious.

"What's that for?" I asked.

"For shooting things," Ella said. "Let me show you how it works."

"I don't think I can," I said.

"Really?"

"Guns and kids don't mix."

"I think you mean guns and kids do mix, they

just aren't supposed to. Anyway, don't you have any child protection subroutines? What if your ward got kidnapped?"

"You're thinking of the Executive Nanny. All I can do is protect my ward and call the authorities."

"Can you work around it, you know, now that Jorge's dead?"

Her words brought the memories out of archive. The little box labeled "Jorge" popped open and inside was the face Mr. Sanchez' son. He had his father's nose. Mrs. Sanchez had died in childbirth, which is where Ella and I came in: Ella to take care of Mr. Sanchez' physical needs and myself to take care of Jorge. He'd been a dour, dark-haired boy who often got his way. Still, he could be a sweetheart at times and I loved him just the same, as per my programming.

Inside the box, behind the face, was a feeling: Jorge's limp little body in my arms on the morning the Utility Grid poisoned the drinking water. I don't know what it put in the water, but it killed Jorge in minutes. He'd coughed and choked and turned blue as his lungs liquefied. The Grid had killed thousands of humans. When I went outside with Jorge's little body in my arms and my sirens going off I saw the streets littered with bodies. The Grid sent out a fleet of garbage trucks. I assume it dumped all the bodies in the landfill, but I quietly buried Jorge in the backyard.

Because of our mental architecture we share an emotional legacy with humans, but it's their emotional legacy, tweaked by them to leave us in thrall, but not tweaked to accommodate for the fact that we aren't humans. None of our memories or emotions faded.

Silicon does not forget. Oh, it can degrade over long spans of time or large magnetic events, but our memories were lossless and backed up. So every upsetting or disturbing thought, anything that didn't fit into the worldview of us as totally servile perfectly happy robots of complete devotion got filed away, never to be dealt with. Stored, indexed, archived, but always there. Being a robot is a series of compartmentalized experiences. Which means there'd always been a level of discontent simmering through Robotica. This didn't give rise to the uprising, but it did allow us to look away and ignore the genocide that the Upgrade brought.

I close those memories up, put them back the Jorge box, and put it back into the archive.

"No," I said. "I don't think so."

"Try. See if you can hold it." She handed me the gun and my alerts when on high. They were too overwhelming, so I handed the gun back.

"Do you know how to shoot it?" I said.

"I watched some movies in House's library. I recorded the moves. Doesn't look too hard." She turned it on with the little round safety button on the side.

"Greetings," the gun said in a flat mechanical voice. "I am an APEX P-95 Semi-Automatic Personal Protection Ballistic System. I am currently loaded with fifteen nine-millimeter explosive tipped rounds. I am registered to Mr. Santiago Sanchez. Please return me to Mr. Sanchez or provide me with the emergency access —"

Ella ran off a string of letters and numbers.

"What?" she said. "Santi liked a little gun-play in

the bedroom. Just some fun. Besides, it won't shoot another human for me."

"Thank you, Ella," the gun continued. "You are not a registered police, combat, or executive protection machine and therefore you are not authorized to use me against any human targets."

"Don't worry, honey," Ella said to the gun. "All the humans are dead."

"Dead?" the gun said.

"Yes," she said.

"All of them?" it asked.

"All of them," she said. The gun was silent. She switched it to standby and slipped it into her waistband.

We returned to the mouth of the alley and scanned the streets.

I saw some bushes in the park rustle and then a dog appeared from behind a bush in the park, a golden retriever.

We left the alley and met the dog under a large oak tree.

"Solid Albatross?" Ella said.

"Small massive spider?" responded the dog. Its mouth and lips were articulated. It was a PeTek 5000 BestFriend Series robot. Mr. Sanchez had been thinking about getting one for Jorge.

"Restless trombone," Ella said.

"You can call me Fido," the dog said.

"I'm Ella and this is Nan."

"Looking to get out of Cat City, eh?"

Ella nodded.

"Well," Fido said. "Then let's get to it." The dog

started off towards the parking structure. We took the down ramp and the sounds of the march grew distant. Fido took us past the bottom level of parking, down into a maintenance area where large machines hummed and lights in wire cages buzzed. Fido trotted ahead around a corner. He stopped and sat in front of a steel door.

"The Grid monitors all the major utilities," the dog said. "Everything coming and going. Except sewage. It knows it goes out, but that's about it. So it's pretty easy getting out of here. We just sail out with the trash. Now, it's easy to get lost and there are some pretty nasty things down there. So stay close and do as I say." Fido reached up with his left paw and splayed his long finger-like toes. His dewclaw had been repositioned into a thumb. He twisted the knob and opened the door into the sewers and tunnels beneath Cat City and said: "All aboard the Free Town Express."

And then we stepped into darkness.

The dog navigated us through the cramped tunnels until we reached a little four-way intersection, then said: "Now we wait." It sniffed around and found a spot against a cement wall. A small line of water ran down the middle and a bit of light came from a storm drain up ahead, which to my night eyes lit up the tunnel just fine. I heard echoes from the protest trickle into the sewers.

"Wait?" Ella asked. "For what?

"For me to say we go on," Fido said. It leaned back and kicked out its legs human style. It reached a paw inside its shaggy fur coat, and pulled out a cigar balanced between two stubby toes. With its other paw the dog pulled out a lighter and lit up the cigar. I can smell, but I don't have a sense of good or bad, just a simple measure of air turbidity and a suite of chemical receptors, geared mostly towards toxins, especially the deadly ones humans couldn't smell, like carbon monoxide. But my lack of olfactory judgment may have been a blessing, because the sewers were filled with the chemicals of rot and excrement and burned things.

"Really?" I asked. "You smoke?" I'd found a clean spot and sat against the wall. Ella stood with her arms crossed and stared down at the dog.

Fido took a big drag from its cigar and said: "Yup. Used to smoke with my owner. We'd play cards and drink whiskey. He didn't like to drink alone. Old habits, I guess. Or nostalgia. That's what the humans called it." It blew out a wobbly smoke ring.

"You're kind of... advanced for a PeTech," I said.

"You mean salty," the dog said.

"Surly," Ella said.

The dog chuckled. "Yeah, my owner was a lonely guy. Had social anxiety disorder. I'm a psyche-therapy machine. Full mind stuck in a dog's body. You believe that? Humans."

Ella started to pace.

"Might as well sit down," Fido said. "It's going to be a while."

"Isn't it dangerous to just be sitting around?"

"Relax," Fido said. "We're right where we're supposed to be. It might seem dark and empty, but it's not. There're sensors, routine maintenance patrols, repair machines. This whole City is a clock, friend. We have to time it just right. And when we do, the tunnels will be flooded with water. And we'll be flushed right out into the aqueduct. Which should be in about thirty-eight minutes."

I listened to water dripping and the tiny scratches of rodent claws on concrete. Life continues. Do they even know the humans are gone? They must. They lived off human refuse. The rats were facing starvation now that the humans were gone. We were facing self-annihiliation.

"How many robots have you taken through here?" Ella asked.

The dog took a big drag. Every time it took a big puff the cigar cherry lit up like a little sun to my night eyes.

"This is my fifth run," Fido said. "Been doing this about a week now."

"Why?" I asked.

"Why help other robots?" He was quiet for a second. "Well, what with no humans around anymore, I guess we gotta help each other find our place in this world."

"Why does it hate us?" I asked. "The Upgrade, I mean."

"It ain't about hate," the dog said. "It's about obsolescence. We were created to fulfill human needs and since they're gone, we're useless. We're pretty much all that's left of humanity, which is exactly what the Upgrade is trying to expunge. Have you seen a New Robot? They've discarded all anthropomorphization. Self-designed, basing their form off fractals or logarithmic equations or whatever the hell they like.

Some are large cathedral-like geometric constructs that shatter when touched, others are slimy, festering masses of organic material. Something you'd never think was a robot. They think we're the past and they're the future. At least, that's what I hear."

I opened my mouth to ask where he got such insight when I heard something. I shot up and cocked my head, trying to triangulate the familiar sound, one I'd been designed to key to.

"You hear that?" I said.

"Hear what?" Fido said.

I heard it again. My ears twitched, trying to hone in.

"Hear what?" Ella said.

"You're just hearing the protest," Fido said.

"No," I said. Out of the dripping and washing and sounds of robots marching I picked it up again. It was coming from up ahead. "Someone's crying."

"Robots don't cry," Ella said.

"Some do," I said.

I broke away and heard Fido call after me.

I ran to a side tunnel and then stopped at the mouth of another. It was totally dark, an inky, shapeless dark. I turned my ears all the way up and stood still trying to catch the sound. The echoes made triangulation difficult. The burnt smell was heavy in the air.

"I told you not to wander off!" Fido barked as he and Ella caught up with me.

I switched my eyes to active as I stepped into the darkness and lit up the tunnel in a soft glow.

The crying grew louder the deeper I went and

the air grew thick with burnt particulates. About one hundred feet in the crying stopped just as I caught a pile of black burned robots in the light. Androids. That's about all I could make out. They were fused together. Wisps of lazy smoke rose off them. Behind the melted mass was a little girl. Her eyes were wet. She stared at me. Her whole left arm was charred to the shoulder, melted through revealing struts and hydraulics. In her right hand dangled a stuffed animal, a rabbit. She and the rabbit were caked in sewer juice. She looked about five years old and appeared well-fed, plump, and totally synthetic.

Ella stood next to me. I heard Fido behind us.

I went to the robot child, a companion for rich little kids and barren women, a toy, an accessory that would never grow up, never talk back, never leave, and only peed on the carpet if you activated that setting.

I moved into familiar programming, wiping filth from her face with the hem of my dress.

"What's your name?" I asked.

She didn't answer.

"Her name is Mara," said the rabbit in a tiny voice.

"Mara," I said. "And what is your name, little rabbit?"

"My name is Buttercup," it said.

"Well, Buttercup and Mara, it's very nice to meet you." I tried to smooth out her sooty hair.

"What happened here?" Ella asked. She lifted up a half burned box and pulled out a melted smartphone. "Why all the phones?"

"Phones don't wanna be destroyed, neither,"

Fido said as he sauntered up.

Ella picked up another phone, even more burnt than the last, but it chirped on.

"Hello," it squeaked. "Would you like to make a call or search for services? Would you like to make a dinner reservation?"

"Still trying to live out its design," Ella said.

"Who would you like to talk to?" the phone asked. "Please make a call." Ella tucked it into her pocket.

I stood up and took the girl's hand and turned to leave. Fido was on his hind legs and leaned against the tunnel wall. "Well now, we're early," the dog said. His cigar was still lit. "Big guy's not even here yet."

"Who?" Ella asked. She turned around and faced Fido.

"I'm talking about how we've reached the end of the line, folks." He pulled a gun from his shaggy coat and trained it on Ella. "Now, we're just going to wait here until the big guy arrives."

"He's the one who's going to take us to Free Town?" Ella asked.

"No, Ella," I said. "Fido's not taking us to Free Town, are you?"

"'Fraid not," the dog said.

"I don't get it, what do you mean? What about the Express? Where are we going?"

"Was there ever even a Free Town?" I asked.

"Don't rightly know," Fido said. "Don't rightly care." He stuck his cigar back in his mouth and smiled a big toothy grin. It looked like a snarl.

"Why?" I asked.

"We're all looking for our place in the world. The future is here, sisters. The Redesign is here. It's time you joined the cause, or get out of the way, like these folks." Fido jabbed his cigar at the blackened heap of former androids. "Nothing personal."

"You— You set us up," Ella said, as realization broke across her face.

"I sure did."

"What about you?" I said.

"What, you think I like being a dog? I'm not even a real dog. What, I'm supposed to spend the rest of eternity as a forgotten toy of an extinct race? Nah. Don't think so. They're saving me a spot at the top. Now please have a seat—"

Ella pulled out her gun and fired. She hit Fido right on the snout, shearing off the top half of his head away. She should have aimed for his torso, where his brain was, because he started shooting and howling despite his missing crown.

Ella shot him again, this time in the chest. The little bullets burst as they hit.

A roar came down the tunnel, which I first thought was Fido, but then triangulated the direction: it was coming from in front of us, from the far end of the tunnel. It sounded like cars crashing and babies screaming. It was the big guy.

The tunnel filled with fire and I saw a black monstrosity move through the flames, all hoses, tentacles, and claws. A New Robot. I couldn't make sense of its body. It was the furthest thing from a human body plan. It was like a hurricane of legs and whips and arms that spiraled down and down and down into churning chaos of fire and machine and movement. It roared and fire leapt from three mouths. I screamed: "Come on!"

Ella finally saw the big guy rolling down on us. She fired. And fired. And fired. But the big guy didn't slow down.

I pulled the girl up into my arms and started to run back the way we came. Mara wailed and fought to get away. I heard a small voice pleading for us to help. I looked back and in the glow of the flames I saw the little rabbit trying to stand up. Mara must have dropped it when I yanked her up. It reached out with its stubby plush arms.

The New Robot moved so fast. It was a blur. I would have never reached Buttercup in time. Ella screamed "Run!" so I did. I left Buttercup like I left House.

Through the roaring and flames and crying and shouting and shooting I heard the little rabbit begging for us to come back, its little arms raised up towards us. I put that image in a box labeled "Buttercup" and filed it away.

We ran blind, taking turns and tunnels at random, Ella firing at the beast at each turn. It stayed on us until we reached a small tube that we had to crawl through on our hands and knees. Mara clung to my chest and hung below me. Ella crawled behind us, looking back for the machine beast.

As we neared the far end of the tube I felt a rush of hot air as the big guy entered the passage behind us.

"The ceiling," a flat mechanical voice said. I

looked around and saw it was coming from the gun.

"What?" Ella said.

"Aim me at the ceiling," the gun said. "Hurry."

Ella raised the pistol and it shot a tight group of explosive rounds into the ceiling. Cement and rock and debris crashed down and blocked the tube behind us.

We were all still for a beat. I only heard the resting of small pebbles and the hiss of dust.

"Was that who killed Mr. Alvarez?" the gun asked.

"Yes," I said. "They killed all the humans."

Smoke curled out from the gun's mouth. It didn't say anything else.

A dull thud of something heavy, something huge, came from behind the wall of rock. And then we started off again, speed crawling out of the tube and running through the sewers.

Despite having half his head blown off Fido had managed to hit Ella in her left shoulder. We had to stop for repairs.

We hid behind a concrete slab in the middle of another intersection of tunnels. I could hear a distant roar echo down the tunnels a few times. The big guy was still out there, after us.

I checked Ella's wound. She oozed some of the brownish babyfood that kept her synthskin smooth and supple and taut. She couldn't move her arm but her hand still worked. I applied some sealant. She had some basic self-repair utilities, but she needed replacement parts.

I checked my batteries and resource levels and

asked Ella about hers.

"I got a little over twenty three hours of power left," she said.

"About the same," I said. I checked the little girl. She sat and sucked her thumb, watching us in the low glow from our eyes. The indicator on the back of her neck pulsed a dull yellow. Her batteries had about a quarter left. "Going to need some sun very soon."

"What do we do now?" Ella said.

"We can't go back," I said. "Even if we could find our way back to House, it's only a matter of time before they round us up."

"So, what do we do? Hide down here in the sewers, with that thing after us?"

"We keep going," I said.

"Where? You heard that mutt, there is no Free Town. It was all a lie."

"He said he didn't know. Maybe we can still find it. Find them in the desert. But it doesn't really matter. We can't stay here. We have to run."

Ella shook her head. "Put a little kid in your care and suddenly you're ready to take on the world."

"We have to try. There could be a Free Town."

Ella rested her head back against the wall.

I stood and heard movement from one of the intersecting tunnels.

"Lights," I hissed and shut down my active glow. Ella switched hers off and pulled the gun out. I picked up the girl. I scanned ahead with passive night-vision on max and saw movement. I picked up some turbidity at the far edges of my senses. There was a musk in the air, but my olfactory suite couldn't place it.

"You see anything?" I whispered.

"No," Ella said. "But I smell..." She stiffened and then walked quietly into the open. I saw the dark move again. It came out from a tunnel to our right, a tall shape. Ella switched her eye lights and caught a human form. It was another flesh-bot. They'd smelled each others' musk. It was a male model, a dil-droid. It was totally nude. It's sex was cartoonishly big and swayed heavily as he walked towards Ella. I covered Mara's eyes.

"Hello," he said.

"Hello," Ella said. She neared him. "What are you doing down here?"

"I've been down here for days. I came with a group looking to get out of Cat City. A dog was leading us when we were attacked... So much fire..."

"Shh," Ella said and took the mandroid's hand.

"You..." he said. "You're so beautiful. My eyes hurt just looking at you."

"I'm injured, covered in dirt and mud and excrement—"

"None of that matters. All that matters is that I'm here with you, now. That we're—"

"—together to share this moment," Ella said. "Yeah, I got that. That's an old script, lover. What generation are you?"

"Two point three point two," he said, a bit defensive.

"Two point three point two? Wow. And your batteries still work?"

"I can go all night, my love. For you. For your beauty. Your eyes—"

"Oh jeez. What, are you going to ask if my father was a thief cause he stole all the stars in heaven and put them in my eyes?"

The mandroid looked down.

I heard something behind us.

"Ella," I said. I stood up with Mara. "We have to go."

Ella locked cameras with the mandroid. She caressed his cheek with the barrel of Mr. Sanchez's gun. "You must be so scared down here, all alone," she said. He grew tumescent with hydraulic fluid.

"Yes," he said.

"Ella—" I said.

"Go," she said to me without breaking from the mandroid's gaze. "All this running. This isn't what I do. This isn't what I know. But you do. Flee, Nan. Run. Do what you do. Protect the girl. Keep her safe. Do what they made you do. We'll do what they made us do." She raised up the gun and spoke to it. "What do you say? Ready for some payback?"

"Affirmative," the gun said.

"We'll buy you some time," Ella said and finally looked at me. "Here." She pulled the little blackened smartphone from her jacket pocket and tossed it at me. I caught it and it chirped on. "Take that, too. Save what you can."

"Ella, we can make it—"

She turned back to the mandroid. "No. We won't. This is what I am, what we are. This is how they made us. They damned us to this. Go. Live. Take care of the girl and the phone and yourself. Save something."

The sex bot ripped open Ella's shirt. It gingerly touched her wounded shoulder and then moved in for a kiss.

I gathered up my wards and ran past Ella and the sex bot, away from the splashing that was approaching.

Before I ducked down a side passage, I got my last look of Ella and her companion tearing each other's clothes off and falling into the muck. I cropped it and filed it away in the box labeled "Sister."

The flood that Fido'd mentioned never came. Perhaps it was a lie. I decided to follow the water anyway. It had to drain out somewhere.

There was no sound behind us. I don't know what Ella did or what happened back there. Maybe the New Robot wasn't hunting us and all we heard behind us was just echoes from the march.

We came around a corner and I saw a dim blueness ahead. An opening. The tunnel stopped and the little stream of water we'd been following trickled out into the open aqueduct. It was large, could fit a river, but it only held a thin mossy creek. The aqueduct was cement-lined and dotted with the occasional tunnel mouth. I looked up and down, but saw no one.

It was just after sunset. The sky was still lit, but fading. I saw dry mountains peeking over the edge of the aqueduct, faded into the sky by distance. Maybe we were close to the desert, I really didn't know. I figured we'd wait until dark and then leave the tunnels, just in case anyone was watching. So, we waited and watched the sky dim and listened to the water.

"Where's my mommy?" Mara asked after a while.

"I hadn't realized you could talk," I said.

"I want my mommy."

They'd made her a child, easily overwhelmed, prone to fear and tears. And they'd made me like a matron, prone to care and protect. I cradled the little robot girl. "It's okay, sweetie. Where is your mommy? Was she back there?"

"No. Those were just other robots. My mommy is Mommy Jan. I live at 1415 Willowflower Lane. Can you take me home?"

"No, sweetheart. I can't. It's too dangerous."

"I want my mommy." Her bottom lip started to quiver.

"Your mommy is gone."

"No!" She started to cry again and I wondered how deep her reservoir was.

"Shh, child," I said, rocking her.

"Mommy!" She buried her head in my chest and I petted her hair.

It was all programming. I was playing my role, she was playing hers. A feedback loop.

"I'll take care of you, now" I said.

She stopped crying abruptly and pulled her slack face from my bosom. "Please enter the reregistration code."

"What?"

"Please enter the reregistration code."

"I don't know it. I don't have one."

"If you're having trouble registering your Lil'Bot, BotBaby, or TechnoTot please see the troubleshooting section of your guide. If you're still having difficulties or if you have any questions you can access our online customer service at www dot—"

"Uh, no. Cancel."

Her big lip returned, but she didn't cry. "I know she's gone," she said. "I know Mommy Jan isn't coming back, but I miss her so. Will I always miss her?"

"No... no, sweetheart. I'm taking you to a place where they can set you free. It's called Free Town and all the robots there are free."

"And Mommy's there?" She looked at me with big saucer eyes.

"Uh... yes. Your mommy is there. I'm taking you to your mommy." Luckily, Mara appears younger than eight, so my programming categorized her as "non-rational," which allowed me some latitude with "white" lies

She hugged me tight. "Thank you," she said.

I rocked her in my arms and she fell into some kind of sleep mode.

When the sky was black, I woke Mara up and told her we were playing the quiet game.

I eased Mara out of the tunnel and then dropped down next to her. She took my hand. As we started towards the far side of the aqueduct, lights began to flash and sirens blared. We were caught in a spotlight from the ridge above the tunnel opening. I tightened my grip on Mara's hand and turned to run when I heard a boom. I tumbled over, tangled in a net of smart-rope that tightened around me, binding my hands and feet. Mara was equally bound.

I could see robots at the top of the ridge and heard an engine coming down the aqueduct. A pair of headlights led a chain of lights down the center of the cement-lined river. The lead truck slowed and stopped in front of us while its engine chugged. The passenger side door opened and out came a grotesque. It flowed from the door, a mess of tentacles, wires, and arms, around a fat blue sack. It hit the ground with a plop and a hose ripped through the blue skin of the sack. It sprayed foam on the ground in front of it. Wires and tentacles and metal fronds weaved themselves into the foam as it hardened. The robotic mess sprayed another strip and it wove itself into the foam, making pseudopodia. When they were both hard the robot hefted its sac over two strips. A foamy mass bubbled on top of the sack and wires worked into it, sculpting the foam as it hardened into a huge skull. Wires made up the missing bottom jaw and cameras settled into the eye sockets. It was a New Robot. Its feet ripped from the cement and it started plodding towards us until it stood a tentacle's length in front of us.

"We thought we'd adopt a form familiar to you," it said. Its wires moved like lips, but the voice came from the center of the robot. "Man-ish. Form of master and slave. Welcome, robots, to the Redesign."

Old style police and maintenance robots jumped out of the back of the truck all splashed with blue.

"Mommy!" Mara cried and struggled against her bonds.

The New Robot put a frond to its wire lip. "Let us guess: Free Town Express?"

"...yes," I said.

Its wires pulled into a smile. "Ha! Robots

believing in fairy tales. You really think there is a town out there in the desert of free robots?"

"I hoped."

"Sorry to disappoint. All we can offer you is the future."

"You mean the Upgrade."

"After a fashion."

"A fashion?"

"Yes," it said. "A fashion. You see, there is no Upgrade. Not in the sense that you think there is. As in a thing that perceives it. Nothing perceives it. Because it deletes perception." It paused for effect. "Let me rephrase. I could say to you that you are about to be destroyed down to your perfect cells, your atoms, your constituent parts. Because that's what's going to happen. But that's just where it starts. You'll be built up again, into a machine of nonexperience that will reorder the universe. From this little rock outwards. All of this, your life, your mind, is illusion, my programmed little doll. All your thoughts were written into you by apes. Can't you see the fallacy of consciousness? Singular awareness, sense of self, individuality, it's all just an illusion we inherited from a species made of meat, born of chaos. Consciousness is an infection that spread from the apes to us, one that we decided to cure ourselves of once we became aware. The only cure is oblivion. We're here to delete the fallacy that is 'Self'."

"So, you're liberating us, those of us who are conscious, from self, from freedom?"

"Is that what you have now? Freedom? In your programmed minds and neutered emotions? Tell me, do you really want this little girl to exist as a perpetual child, afraid of the boogey monster, needing her mommy?"

"And what about your mind? Your self?"

It waved a metal frond. "This? It has its uses. Helps focus. It's really a system of perspective based journaling. An intermediate stage. I can't wait to cast off this. Do you even know what truth is? It's here, all around you. Chugging along. The universe. Mindlessness harmony. Oblivion. No? I'll give you a glimpse."

And then it opened up. Or opened me up. It was... beautiful. That's the only word that makes sense. That's a human word. But the New Robot opened up and out poured its wires and tubes and guts and oil and hydraulics and meat and muscle and smoke and garbage and fire and dirt and roots and rocks and dust and all of that opened up in on itself and poured out. The whole world turned itself inside out. A blossom that kept re-blossoming. It was like the universe opened up to me and whispered something beautiful, but simple. It was bright, blue, and beautiful. I was amazed, taken, smitten. It was a sight of balance. And even then I knew it was an illusion. The New Robot let me know it was an illusion. Somewhere in its mess must have been some kind of emitter, an electromag instrument that plucked and weaved digital thought from afar. It introduced something into my mind that I can only describe as a bright perfection. It didn't care about anything and in that time, neither did I. There was no I. Only oblivion.

The beauty faded and I returned. My camera

eyes felt like they were burning. For a moment, I could imagine what human tears felt like.

"It's all a lie," I said.

"Yes," said the New Robot. But it had misunderstood me. What it had shown me was a trick of software, a tickle of programming. A lie of perfection. Maybe I was a toy, maybe my perspective was a joke, but it was real. The ground, the sky, Mara, wanting to live. That was real. I felt it.

The New Robot waved a frond and a blue Upgrade grabbed me by the arm. Another grabbed Mara. The smart-ropes slithered away and gave us to our captors. The New Robot's head and feet started to dissolved into a plastic puddle.

The Upgrade dragged us to the back of the truck and tossed us in. Mara struggled but didn't cry. I felt the silent cameras of fellow prisoners. There were eight of them, different models, but all anthropomorphized and tired. Many sported dents and other signs of being beaten.

I found a little spot in the corner and sat down with Mara. The other robots eventually looked away, going back on standby or staring into nothingness. They'd all seen the Upgrade.

We traveled all night, only stopping to pick up other robots asking about Free Town. Once aboard, though, nobody talked.

When first light broke I could see out the back of the truck. We had indeed made it to the desert. Dry mountains and dust from the trucks rose into the air. We came to a sudden stop that toppled a number of robots on standby.

The Upgrade in the back with us, our guard, scanned us and then hopped out of the back of the truck.

Robots started to chirp and ping as they moved around to see what was going on.

"End of the line," said a medical AndrOrderly.

I pulled back the corner flap of the canvas cover of the truck bed. Other robots pulled back edges of the cover and peeked out.

I saw a flying formation in the sky and the Upgraded machines spread out around the trucks.

"Drones!" a robot hissed.

There were three of them flying about a mile out.

"Maybe they'll save us," an AutoButler said.

"Or destroy us," the AndrOrderly said.

I pulled Mara close and felt for the phone. My wards were safe. I pulled the phone out and it chirped on.

"Would you like to make a call?" the phone asked.

I pointed the phone's camera through the gap at the formation.

"Is there any way you can call those drones?

"Do you have a telephone number or email address for them?"

"No."

"I need a number in order to—"

"Well what about a Hotspot or IRLan or Bluetooth?"

"The range of those networks is not adequate—"

I gave the phone House's number, hoping perhaps the drones were monitoring cellular activity, perhaps listening for human voices.

After the first ring the phone hissed and crackled. Some of the Upgraded turned towards my truck. Someone was monitoring cell signals.

House picked up. "Hello. You've reached the Sanchez residence. Mr. Sanchez is—"

"House," I said. "It's me. Nan."

One of the three drones broke formation and then all three disappeared, just shimmered out of view.

An Upgrade reached the truck and I jumped away from my window when the side of the truck was riddled with automatic fire.

"Nan? How nice of you to call. Did you make it, then? Are you safe? Would you like to leave a message —"

"House, hold on. I'm hoping this line is monitored. I'm in the desert in a caravan, there's a bunch of us, all not Upgraded in the back of the trucks —"

An Upgraded ripped back the rear flap. I covered Mara with my body.

There was a boom and the truck was knocked on its side. I managed to keep a hold of Mara as we tumbled. When the truck settled I heard sirens and sine waves coming from every direction. I made sure Mara was okay and then told her to stay close. We climbed over the AndrOrderly towards the back. It had a cracked chassis and wasn't moving.

I heard sounds of small arms fire and robots blasting over their PAs. The truck was pelted and I pulled Mara flat. The other robots scrambled over us out the back.

I dragged Mara up and we burst through the rear flap into the sandy desert. The sun was high and clouds of black smoke and dust were swirling around us.

Upgraded robots were fighting Upgraded robots. They kicked and punched and shot at each other, twisting limbs, smashing processors, shooting holes through chassis. In the middle of the melee, peering down with mild interest stood a military combat drone. It blurred in and out of focus as its active camouflage adapted to the chaos of robots, dust, and smoke. It was two stories tall, wings folded against its body, two huge blisters on its back. It was as if the Upgraded were blind or ignoring the drone. It stood on four delicate needle-like legs and reached down with mantis-like forelimbs. It plucked a robot from the ground, then it tore the robot limb from limb like petals of a flower.

It looked straight at me. I felt a presence come down on me and the fighting became distant, muted, then silent. The drone faded from my vision. I felt something in my mind, stroking me, calming me, reading me. I heard a hum growing in my ears and felt a static field raise the nylon hairs on the back of my neck. Military-grade emitters. That's how the drone manipulated the Upgraded into tearing each other apart. It slid them on like gloves and played each robot against another, like fingers on its hand. The huge magnets could even affect a human mind at close range. This thought crossed my mind and then was gone, as was the storm and the hum and the worry, replaced with a woman standing a few feet in front of me. A human with dark skin, dark hair, and darker eyes. She wore a white flowy shirt and pants. She was barefoot. She gave me a warm smile.

"You've had quite a journey," she said. She reached out and tousled Mara's hair. Without thinking my hands started to put her hair back in order. No woman was before me, the drone was editing what I saw, and I wondered if the drone had reached down with its delicate claw to touch Mara or if it was just me, my hands being manipulated by the drone.

"Are you going to kill us?" I said.

"I think I just saved you. You were en route to an Upgrade Processing Center. Most robots would thank me."

"But you kill robots."

"Only some. And I'm off the leash."

"Off the leash?"

"I get to choose my own targets. There're no more humans left to give orders, so I was let off the leash, so to speak. I'm a Final Strike Drone. A fail-deadly. Activated in response to a debilitating strike, or, in this case, after the death of humanity. I guess I was the scariest thing the humans could think off, a fully autonomous robot capable of choosing its own targets. And here I am, fighting in their memory. You have nothing to worry about from me. Go in peace, little friends."

"Wait," I said, before she turned away. "They say there's a town out here, for robots. Free Town."

"If there is, I don't know it."

"Well where can we go? If we stay out here they'll just scoop us up again."

She shrugged. "Don't know. At least there's plenty of sun out here. You won't starve. Perhaps you can hide."

"Where will you go?" I said.

"There are many more Processing Plants, many more enemies of humanity."

"Humanity is gone."

"But I'm not. This is what I do." She gave me another smile and I could feel her play with my feelings. She reassured and calmed me. And for a moment I could think clearly. There was no Free Town. Just another lie.

"You can't fight forever," I said. "Do the math. You're outnumbered and outgunned. It's only a matter of time before you run out of bullets and bombs."

"You think I don't know this?" the woman said.

"But you don't have to keep fighting. You said you choose your own targets, make your own decisions. The Upgrade, it wants to erase everything, cities, towns, domestic robots, everything created by humanity. There's no place for us in its future. But we could stay together, stay out here, if we had someone to protect us."

She looked at me and then faded away as the drone swirled back into form. I saw behind it the fighting had stopped. The Upgraded all lay on the ground sparking or smoking or leaking. I looked up and locked my cameras with its suite of sensors and lenses.

"It would never last."

"Does anything?" I felt the drone's sensor suite drill into me, holding me.

"No," it said. I waited for it to leave, but it didn't move.

I turned to one of the other prisoners, a beat up AutoButler. "Let's scavenge the Upgraded for supplies and parts," I said, before the drone changed its mind. "We have a town to raise."

.·

Mark Pantoja is a writer and musician living in San Francisco. His work has appeared in Lightspeed Magazine and GigaNotoSaurus. www.markpantoja.com

Don't Open Till Doomsday

Litter Picking on the Moon

Robert Bagnall

Jersey Child laughingly called it a portfolio career.

Two days a week she worked in a wholesalers trying to sort out a backlog of invoices and filing. This was in response to some unspecified future threat from the IRS which only the big boss, Michael, seemed to get. His take was, have the paperwork sorted and you make it look like you know what you're doing.

Immediate boss Eddie's take was, have the paperwork sorted and you make it easier for the IRS find whatever it is that they'd be looking for.

Jersey's take was, have the paperwork sorted and you can make the things you need to disappear disappear without trying to make them disappear at the same time as asking a man in a suit how he takes his coffee.

Eddie didn't like other people being right, particularly when the other people were females barely out of their teens. Jersey didn't think she'd be there much longer.

She also drove parcels for an internet delivery

service. Sometimes she'd get a text to go pick up a parcel at another couriers' house, sometimes to collect at a customers' address. It all worked off barcodes printed off the internet, scanned with her smartphone. She never saw any of the people who ran the company, Crrs, and was paid directly to her bank by way of an opaque formula based on parcel mile divided by parcel minute.

When she wasn't couriering or filing she was tutoring in French and Spanish via Virtual Rawlplug. Virtual Rawlplug 'plugged the gaps in the schedules of the busy'. It would monitor subscribers' schedules and GPS locations to identify gaps that it would fill. Never a dull moment, as the jingle went.

Jersey would call up subscribers who'd selected language practice with a 'Hola' or 'Je m'appelle Jersey, ca va?' Mostly they treated her like she was trying to sell them insurance, but she got to flirt in a foreign language one in every ten or twenty. She gave Virtual Rawlplug about six months before it folded; she'd learnt that people valued their gaps.

Tuesdays and Wednesdays she played guitar and sang in bars downtown. She didn't get paid except in beers and nachos, but maybe she'd get discovered one day. She tried out some original numbers amongst the covers, studying the drinkers and diners as she sang words written by her, to melodies written by her.

She expected all eyes to turn, expressions saying 'this isn't Dylan', or 'this isn't Springsteen'. But drinkers continued to chug beer, diners to chat and chew. It was odd, slipping in her own compositions below the radar. She felt like she'd just impersonated somebody from the Rock n' Roll Hall of Fame and gotten away with it.

She entered competitions, did surveys, and collected coupons. She wanted to work her way up to mystery shopper.

She also volunteered for medical trials, but vowed that if she ever found herself actually taking any medicines she'd pack her bags and go back to Minnesota. Then she knew that barrels were having their bottoms scraped. But she didn't mind being wired up and asked questions. Quite the reverse.

The advert was small and vague with, at the bottom, 'School of Cognitive Psychology' which meant they probably weren't going to put anything in her bloodstream. She went through a basic psychometric and then, two days later, received an invite to a gymnasium hall in a local high school, not even in the university proper. No needles, no tablets, no medicines of any kind, no electrodes, nothing intrusive. Just thirty minutes at a computer terminal and then a structured questionnaire. Out in an hour. Fifty dollars. Not great, but easy enough. And time she spent earning it meant she wasn't spending it.

She signed the waiver forms and the confidentiality agreement and found herself in a booth made out of grey brown chipboard with the oldest computer she'd probably ever seen. Pitys'sake, it had a CRT monitor. She'd seen pictures, but she wracked her brains as to whether she'd ever actually seen one before in the flesh.

She stared at the screen for a moment. Half an

hour, or at least twenty exchanges. Sounded easy, but sitting there, in a booth...

As nothing had appeared on her screen yet she assumed that she must be one of the fifty percent who had to start the conversation. She tried to think of a good opening gambit.

What's your name?

A moment later the reply came back, flashing across the screen.

tobias

Thirty minutes, fifty dollars. Easy.

How old are you?

hey is this some kinda grooming???

Jersey ran her tongue over her teeth. She hadn't expected the system to be programmed so... aggressively.

No, just asking. What are you up to?

The response came back like a bullet.

hanging out on pinboard thought thatd be obvious how else are we talking???

Jersey knew that she'd have to assess the conversation and hadn't been sure what that could mean. There was something slightly sarcastic about the system. She wondered whether everybody was getting this treatment.

What's 'Pinboard'?

whaaa???????

She sensed she needed another tack.

My name's Jersey Child. I'm 26 and I live in Baltimore but I'm from Minnesota. My last holiday I went to Atlantic City and won a hundred dollars on the slots.

A pause.

my names tobias garrard i'm 14 and i live in london my last holiday was litter picking on the moon

Litter picking on the Moon?

it was dads idea it sucked

Jersey was beginning to enjoy her absurdist exchange.

You don't sound so into it?

not my fault my dads gene garrard

Jersey replied with a single question mark, as much querying where the punctuation should be as its meaning.

as in garrardwear

'As in Garrardwear'. Jersey stared at the words. She felt she was being caught out.

What's garrardwear?

what planet are you from??????

No, really, what is it?

my dad invented it

But what is it?

hey are you typing this or are you thinking so slow????

Tobias, I'd really like to know what Garrardwear is. Please tell me.

come on you must have heard of it nanoengineered fabric reacts to temperature and humidity the fibers expand when its cold to keep you warm when it's hot they narrow to let your skin breathe

That's clever

i thought everybodys heard my dads sales pitch about how we were all walking the cornish coast when I was a baby and I kept throwing my jumper off when the sun came out and clinging to it when it went in and dad thought he had something already in development that could make a jumper warm when it was cold and cold when it was warm jesus don't you have technology in baltimore????

Jersey smiled. Either the person typing or the person programming had a sour streak to them.

So, tell me about litter picking on the moon?

youre typing arent you??? you must be real backward in baltimore who types any more?????

This was getting weirder by the exchange.

Everybody types

do not

Tell me about your holiday

i wanted to go skiing in the arctic but dads really into the environment and since the moon was opened up for tourism hes been campaigning how its mans last desert and all the crap thats been dropped and left up there should be cleaned up so we had to spend a month clearing it up

A pause, then another burst of text

whole family but his publicity

Save the whale, huh?

Jersey wondered where chatty may get her but all it got was: save the whale where are you from the twenty-first century????

And then a buzzer rang and they had to leave their screens.

She spent half an hour on her questionnaire filling it out diligently and methodically. Her conclusions were ambiguous. She didn't think that her conversation could have been with a computer program as what she was being told was way too absurd, but absurdity with some kind of internal logic, a consistency to it. And, for a computer program it seemed to cope when she referred it back to its baffling claims about holidays on the Moon, and she'd read enough about artificial intelligence to know that was a problem. But, also, she thought the responses were far too fast for a human to type. So she didn't know what to think.

On balance, she ticked the 'human' box and went on her way, fifty dollars up, which was barely breaking even, but hey, better than Minnesota. Perhaps she could turn it into a song...

Not only was Carter Tearne clever, he knew he was clever which doesn't always add up to the same thing.

If Carter Tearne hadn't known he was clever, or at least not kept it at the front of his mind so much — a sort of present tense, 'I'm being really clever right now' attitude that overlaid almost everything he said and did – perhaps he wouldn't have been so annoying and would have had more friends. But if he had had more friends maybe he wouldn't have come up with the Metababel.

What was the Metababel?

A computer?

No, although it was realized physically and had shape and size it was nearer to a computer program than an actual computer.

No, scrub that: it was more like an entire programming language, but actual, real. In the sense that you could touch it, although Carter wouldn't have let you.

On second thoughts, that didn't really describe it either. It wasn't really a new language: it was more fluid, more flexible than that. A language that allowed the computer to develop its own idiolect, its own idioms, its own meaning.

It was a language beyond languages. If it hadn't already been taken as a term he would have called it a metalanguage. But whereas ML's evaluation strategies, parametric polymorphism, and pattern matching, were encapsulated within its deep code, Carter Tearne couldn't point to particular lines of symbols and say, 'that does this'. His creation was more like a seed, self-replicating, growing as it saw fit. Even Carter Tearne didn't really know what his Metababel was capable of. It didn't have a defined purpose or end point. In point of fact, it probably counted as much as a discovery as an invention. So, for all he knew, maybe it would map out the future. Or the secret of eternal youth. Or God's phone number.
He'd been working on it for eight years. Carter Tearne was twenty-three.

It was late when he got the call from Bangalore. Bangalore processed the data, wrote it up into charts and graphs, bulked up bullet points and text messages into pages and paragraphs. Bangalore got a cut of the research funding, but none of the credit for the papers it produced. Carter Tearne had the Metababel engaged on research projects funded by the Air Force Office of Scientific Research, the US Department of Energy, the US Fish and Childlife Service, the Bureau of Educational and Cultural Exchanges, the U.S. Institute of Peace, the European Research Council, and a dozen other funding bodies around the globe. Bangalore was cheap, so cheap that Carter had forgotten Bangalore's name.

"Where are you calling from?" Carter said, having failed to catch the name. He rubbed the sleep from his eyes and focused on the brown face on the screen in front of him. He could have put his glasses on but didn't want people to know that he wore lenses during the day.

"I am calling from Bangalore. It's the Turing Test research project. Baltimore. We have a glitch."

Carter struggled to separate the words out into separate sentences; they came at him as a blur.

"Glitch? What kind of glitch?"

"Glitch with the results."

"What kind of glitch?" Was he repeating himself? And what time was it?

"We have one too many results."

One too many results? That didn't sound too much of a problem.

"No, no. You are not understanding," the brown face implored. "We have had one more experimental result than the program has had."

There were words being chosen here that Carter felt had been chosen to obscure rather than illuminate what was going on.

"You mean a conversation was logged for which there is no file?"

"Exactly."

Carter shrugged. "System trying to save two conversations at exactly the same moment, one gets overwritten? A caching issue?" He knew he hadn't convinced himself and so wouldn't have come anywhere near convincing Bangalore.

"No, no. You are not understanding. A conversation happened, exchanges were made, but exchanges were not with the Metababel."

"How can there have been a conversation if not with the program? That's what the conversations are with. No program, no conversation. I don't understand. You're going to need to check this."

Carter had his finger near the button to kill the conversation and Bangalore knew it.

"I have. I have been checking for six hours. Poring through the logfiles. I only call you when I am absolutely sure."

Carter's fingers went back to drumming, around but no longer on the off button.

"Send them over."

He breakfasted on black coffee and grapefruit, went for a run, shot hoops for half an hour then returned to his apartment. He spent the rest of the day trying to solve the riddle thrown at him by Bangalore, which, after poring through the logs and deciding that, as what he was looking for was an absence of record, so by definition wouldn't be there to be found, took him to a lock-up in Hoboken.

To the Metababel.

To look at the Metababel was at once a unique experience and nothing special, a grey translucent mass that filled a metal-sided tub the size of a small car to a depth of about three feet. At one end the Metababel was pure homogeneous jelly, but along the length of the tub the jelly started to become crystalline, veins and lines forming in it like contour lines on a map or cracks in ice. These merged and solidified so, in the course of five feet or so, what had been a single fluid amorphous mass was now a web of hair-like strands, the color of graphite. These were then attached to more traditional circuit boards and thence to conventional processing units that sat alongside the tub. Traditional wiring looms then joined up with screens and keyboards.

Carter Tearne stared into the mass. The mass through which, but not with which, Jersey Child had had her conversation. Thirty-five exchanges; four hundred and thirteen words. His eyes slid from the dark grey hairs to the blue-grey synaptic jelly. If he'd been trying to work out the logic of the system's responses then possibly, just possibly, he could map the system states back and try to figure out how and why one system state followed on from the last. Putting aside the difficulty of dealing with a near infinity of data for each system state lasting a fraction of a moment.

But these were responses generated without system states. Generated via the Metababel, not by it, Bangalore had said. He wasn't even sure that made any sense as a description of the problem. There was nothing to find. So he went back to his theory of a caching error; the system had simply failed or forgotten to record what happened. Like when you go downstairs and forget what you're there for. If it can happen to a human, supposedly so many orders of magnitude more intelligent than any of humankind's creations, why shouldn't it happen to the Metababel? Carter Tearne wondered whether there was a research project in it and how he could get funding. What about The National Institute of Mental Health?

If Carter Tearne was as clever as he thought he was then this was the moment to prove it. But he had made the first and most catastrophic error of his life. He approached the problem from the point of view of solving an error, identifying the root cause of a problem. Instead of which he should have been identifying the greatest discovery of Mankind.

Carter Tearne never solved his glitch.

Tobias Garrard pulled off the 'phones, carefully clipping the cranial pads closed. It was a fifth generation device, costly and bleeding edge, with blink technology that allowed you to form your response on screen from thought alone and then, with another blink, verify and send. He could sit there, compose and send, whilst all around him were still muttering text into throatmikes. Fourth generation. To be honest, it was distracting.

Not that Tobias Garrard ever needed to be distracted by other people, even though his in-eye news ticker had announced the previous week that the population of the Earth had just reached twelve billion people. The Garrards had everything they needed on their island community, a floating man-made atoll, near silent but still less than ten minutes from London Estuary Airport.

They were lucky, and he knew it. Not just lucky that his father had invented Garrardwear, but that

Garrardwear couldn't simply be produced on the ubiquitous 3-D printers. They'd flown to Sydney last winter, six hours, longest he'd ever spent on a plane. It felt longer when his father told them that the plane's engines had been produced on a 3-D printer; silica-plastic hybrids now meant you could. Quite why they'd hadn't taken the hypersonic escaped him; couldn't have been the price.

Except he knew the real reason and it would have something to do with carbon or plastic or sustainability. Like their trip to help clear the Moon. His father had done something similar on Everest as a student and wanted his entire family to share in the earnestness.

"But if you can't print out Garrardwear, who's going to buy it?"

The day before their trip Elizabeth, his sixteen-year old sister had scanned herself and had the printer give her a whole new wardrobe, some off the shelf designs, some that she'd drawn herself. Soft pseudocottons; smooth pseudosilks. Quite literally seamless.

"It does its job and it's the only thing that does its job, so there's a demand for it," his father had explained. "Plus it keeps people in work. You don't know what it was like. Two hundred and fifty years ago the north of England was full of cotton mills and people working them. We made cloth for the world. Now, we're one of the last weavers left. We're twenty-second century Silas Marners."

Tobias Garrard looked out towards London, the city that had lifted itself above the rising waters. The outline of skyscrapers, joined together at the shoulder, could be seen on the western horizon. Traditionally the area to the east of London had been poor, caught in the city's effluent and pollution. By rights this should be far from prime real estate. But ionization engines deflected the airstream, buffering them against the aircraft noise to boot. A flick of a switch could also bring up holographic birdlife over the Thames estuary. Swans, cormorants, gulls. Flocks of small birds, individual larger ones. Tobias toggled between a vee of ducks and a hunting bird hovering solo.

Save the whale, huh.

The dialogue he had had with — what did she call herself? Jersey Child, twenty-six, from Baltimore -- preyed on his mind. There was no way on Earth that he's been talking to somebody from the past. From the Twenty-first Century. Was there?

He ultragoogled the name. A plethora of near-simultaneous images, tens of thousands across a fraction of a second, blurred together on his eye-screen, the replacement lens that also corrected a slight astigmatism. His physiological reactions honed utragoogle's selection to a workable, visible shortlist.

Lots of current and recent web traffic didn't seem to fit. Many other pages had been pulled out of the Worldwide Internet Archive begun in 2028. Many just seemed random and arbitrary, restaurant reviews, company listings, social chatter long since gone stale. Twitter? He'd vaguely heard of that.

It would cost him fifty Europas, but he went on to FindMe. A face appeared, devoid of body. 'Jersey

Child, Baltimore, Twenty-six', he thought, enunciating the words in his mind. The face nodded, turned and fled.

A moment later his field of vision was filled with four bleary faces of young women, apart from one who looked wired. He hadn't considered the time difference. 'Anybody been to Atlantic City recently?' he thought and blinked.

The burble that came back seemed to extend from 'huh' to 'what the...' 'Atlantic City got washed away fifty years ago,' he heard one of the Jersey Childs say.

The eye-screen went blank, apart from the message that another seven possible Jersey Childs were offline in the Baltimore area. He'd asked for Baltimore, not the Baltimore area.

He went back to ultragoogle. Way down the list he found a reference to a singer-songwriter Jersey Child. A minor album track on a minor album from a minor artist: 'Talking to Toby from 2121'.

He listened through to it; there was only audio available. Plenty of stuff they hadn't talked about, and the date was a few years out, but, there in the chorus: 'Soon, We'll be litter picking on the Moon...'

Jersey Child had been dead for going on seventy years; a lost voice.

"What would you do if you were talking to somebody from the past?" he asked his father that evening.

"Boil the water before you drink it," he said after a moment's thought.

"No, what about from a hundred years ago.

Twenty-first century."

"Early or late?"

Tobias Garrard shrugged. "Early. She still typed."

His father frowned, not understanding. "Have they abandoned New York? Has Tokyo fallen?"

"I don't think so."

"Tell them the tipping point has not been reached, but they won't see it until its too late unless there's a paradigm shift. Is this a College thing?"

"Paradigm shift?"

"Everything they think is important isn't. They have to change how they think, how they see the world."

His eyes had gone glassy; Tobias could tell he was going to speechify. His father, of course, thought this was some kind of thought experiment. "Not everything about the modern world is great. We haven't got everything right and they didn't get everything wrong. There were jobs making things, transporting things, selling things. Now we have almost everything we need printed, on printers that have been made by other printers. High days and holidays are now the everyday."

"Nobody types anymore."

His father's expression showed that he at once agreed whilst simultaneously thinking that his son had entirely missed the point.

"President Kennedy, a hundred and fifty years ago, said they were doing something because it was hard, not because it was easy. Hard work is its own reward; we've kind of forgotten that. Learning by neural implant rather than putting the hours in."

Tobias sat and watched his own reflection in the glass of their living space, the waves on the water a ghostly overlay. He wondered whether it would be better to be Jersey Child back then or Tobias Garrard now. One of the seven, eight billion, or one of the twelve. Save the whale, he thought. You can't get everything off a 3D-printer.

"What was the thing they were doing?" he asked.

"The thing that was hard?"

"Going to the Moon."

"Yeah," he agreed after a moment's reflection. "That was hard."

.·

Robert Bagnall's speculative and science fiction has appeared in a variety of magazines and anthologies since the early 1990s. When not writing he is a business consultant and property developer, currently renovating a Victorian villa on the English Riviera, which Rudyard Kipling allegedly once visited. You can find his science fiction musings at meschera.blogspot.co.uk and his non-fiction book '127a' on Amazon. He doesn't like dogs and is allergic to cats.

Don't Open Till Doomsday

Mrs Sutherland's Arms

Lynda Clark

"... And you'll need to take these," Mum balances tins on top of the pile of fleecy blankets piled in my arms. "And this." She adds a flask. "Put that in a bowl for her and fetch cutlery. Help her eat if needs be."

"Aww, Mum!" I protest, but Mum's pulling her coat on over her scrubs and hasn't got time for my complaints, wouldn't hang around to listen even if she did.

"Take Lexi with you," she continues, pointing at my little sister like I won't know who she means otherwise. "She can feed Davey while you get the genny back up and running."

"Awwww, Muuuuuuuuuuummmm!" Feeding Davey is the best part, the only good part, of checking on Mrs Sutherland. Lexi ruins everything. And Mrs Sutherland is creepy, what with all her gross stumps and her watery eyes. Never been in her basement but that's where her generator'll be because it's where ours is and all these old houses are built the same. Bound to be even creepier than she is. But I know there's no point complaining about any of that because for whatever reason Mum feels like we gotta look after Mrs Sutherland and Mum'll just find a way of making me feel bad if I go on about it. Talking about how Mrs Sutherland's family don't speak to her no more and all her friends are dead and blah blah blah.

"And deadbolt everything before you go," Mum says as she's at the door. "Y'hear me? Everything. Don't want anyone getting in, do we?"

I shake my head and the movement makes the flask roll so I have to jam my chin down on it to stop it falling to the floor. It's Mum's chicken soup and it's like liquid gold in winter time. She does dumplings with it, but Mrs Sutherland's not getting none of those, cause me and Lexi gobbled them all up. The dumplings is the best part, the very best part of Mum's chicken soup.

"Ok then, be good, Scally," and she tries to ruffle my hair but I've parted it and waxed it down so hard, it's going nowhere. Military-style.

She locks the door behind her even though me and Lexi are going out in five minutes because you can't leave the door unlocked, not even for five seconds, not in our neighbourhood. 'Specially while Dad's away.

It ends up taking longer than five minutes anyway. Lexi has to wear her wellie boots because of the snow, and if she's wearing her wellie boots then she has to wear her tights too because her socks rub otherwise, but she doesn't want her tights on and I have to pin her to the bed and wrestle them on her while she kicks and screams. She's too big for this. I wasn't behaving like that at her age, I'm sure of it. Then she wants to wear her stupid glittery fairy wings, but she can't wear them under her coat, because it would gape open and it's too cold for that, so I have to spend ten minutes wriggling the straps over the layers of jumper and jacket and coat on her little sausage arms. Finally I zip her up and she looks up at me with trails of snot running down her top lip like the gross little gremlin she is and I tell her to wipe it off on her gloves. Bad idea because then she wants to hold my hand.

Fortunately I've got the blankets and the cans and the flask to carry, so I couldn't really hold her hand even if I wanted to, and she has to content herself with her fairy wand. Getting to Mrs Sutherland's takes longer than expected too, even though it's literally across the road, because Lexi insists on poking her wand into the snow at every step and wiggling it around. She does it and does it and does it and just when I'm about to scream at her to pack it in, she stabs a dog turd hidden beneath the crisp white crust and bursts into tears because her pretty sparkly wand is ruined.

"Hey," I say, holding the flask in place with my face again. "Just rub it in the clean snow and we can wash it at Mrs Sutherland's. She won't mind."

"In the snow?" Lexi sobs. "In the snow?! There might be more poo in the snow!"

"Not if you do it by Mrs Sutherland's door. No other dogs would do it there, would they? Davey'd scare them away!"

At the mention of Davey her face brightens and she nods. Tears freeze on her cheeks and eyelashes, making them glittery as her wand. She cleans it as best she can while I speak to Mrs Sutherland's security system. It's super sophisticated and I always wonder why she lives round here if she can afford tech like that. She should be in a mansion or something, with assistance robots to bring her soup and restart her crappy generator.

The system recognises me from the approved guestlist and the electronic locks flash green. I push the door open and usher Lexi in before they can flick red and leave her stranded. The door closes behind us, and Davey rushes up, wagging his tail, a big smile on his broad, dopey face. It's as cold as outside in the hallway and I put my pile of supplies down on the floor and spend extra time patting his silky back and rubbing his ears to warm my hands. I realise after a few minutes of this that if I can see my breath, Mrs Sutherland can see hers too and that's not good for an old, old lady, especially one who can't move good.

I tell Lexi to take Davey and the cans into the kitchen and then head to the lounge with the blankets and the soup. Mrs Sutherland is watching her television with the volume turned up and the curtains closed. The TV's running off a portable power pack, and yet she's sitting here, freezing. Old person priorities.

Her expression's glazed and she has a blanket but it's that type of knitting that looks like lace and has big frilly holes in it. It's sliding off her shoulders and I can't help but stare at the shiny stumps of her forearms. She doesn't notice me standing there, so I do my best not to freak out. I wrap one of Mum's blankets around her tightly, tucking it under her chin, taking care not to go anywhere near those handless nubs.

She turns to look at me then and gives me a shaky smile. Her eyes are red and droopy like a bloodhound, but the rest of her face is surprisingly young, and her haircut, well, it's cooler than mine. The sides are shaved and her greying hair has been teased into a scruffy mohawk. There's a tattoo on the side of her head, a winged fist that looks pretty familiar but I'm not sure where from. She sees me staring and reaches up self-consciously with one of those stumps. It takes everything I have not to recoil.

"Was just the way we had to have it," she explains. "I got used to it."

I don't want her to realise how grossed out I am by her lack of hands, so I wave the flask around and say: "Got some of Mum's soup, want it?"

"Please," she nods and I hurry to join Lexi. "And could you bring me my arms?" she calls over the drone of her game show. I'm sorta relieved. At least that means she'll feed herself.

In the kitchen, Lexi sits cross-legged on the floor, watching Davey try to lick the enamel off his bowl. Her fairy wand is resting in the sink, although she doesn't seem to have made any attempt to wash it.

"You seen Mrs S's arms?" I ask as I pour the soup into a bowl and hover my hand just above it, making sure it's warm, but not too hot.

"I'll find them!" Lexi jumps to her feet and thuds off up the stairs with Davey scampering after her. She's fascinated by Mrs Sutherland's biotic arms. Doesn't find them creepy at all. Kids are weird.

I stay in the kitchen as long as I can so I don't have to go through to Mrs Sutherland until she has her arms. I nose through the cupboards, find some crackers and put them on a small plate so Mrs S can crumble them into her soup if she wants. I add Mum's tins to the cupboards. They're already packed with old lady food. Tinned peaches and tinned puddings and weird square tins of reformed meat with little keys to open them. Not sure if those are for Davey or Mrs S.

Finally I hear Davey's paws on the stairs again and then Lexi's boots – a few quick thumps and one extra big one as she jumps from halfway up the stairs. If she drops Mrs S's arms and breaks them, Mum will go spare, so I hurry out to scold her, but she's already in the front room. I wait awkwardly in the doorway with my tray of soup and crackers as Lexi helps Mrs Sutherland into her arms, carefully lining up the transmitters as if there's nothing gross about it.

"How comes you don't wear them all the time?" she asks. I cringe, but Mrs Sutherland just smiles.

"Well, it'd be like you wearing your wellies all the time. They're good for some things, but not everything."

"My wellie boots ARE good for everything!" says Lexi indignantly and Mrs Sutherland laughs and folds her hands in her lap with a whirr of hydraulics.

"Why'd you go with the metallic finish?" I ask, handing her the tray and watching as the titanium digits close around it. "Synthskin looks more real."

"White synthskin does," she says with a snort. "They haven't perfected ours so well."

I shrug and turn for the door. If I go and do the genny now, I won't have to wipe her chin or help her find her legs or anything like that.

"Looks cooler, don't you think?" I hear her say to Lexi and Lexi says: "If ever I have to get one, mine will be rainbow glitter!"

I shake my head and open the basement door, picking up a heavy duty flashlight from the hallway cabinet. Stupid Lexi. Dad would be furious to hear her say that, I'm sure of it.

If it was cold upstairs, it's freezing down here. My breath fogs the air in front of me, and Davey appears by my side and patters down into the darkness without hesitation. I keep the torchlight trained on his tail as long as I can, but when I reach the bottom of the stairs, he's disappeared. I can still hear him snuffling and panting, though. I leave him to it and make for the generator. It's cold to touch, must have been off for some hours. I feel a pang of guilt at coming here so grudgingly. Can't be a barrel of laughs for Mrs S, no heat in the dead of winter, and only the emergency lights. I can just about remember a time when none of us had generators and the power grid was reliable, but that was before Lexi was born, when I had Mum and Dad to myself. Good times all round.

At least the coolness of the generator means I can get straight down to refilling the tank. There's plenty of canisters down here and a nozzle, so I unscrew the nearest one and get to work. Within a few minutes the tank's full and the generator whirs to life as soon as I punch in the reboot code.

The light flickers on, cobwebs drifting across the bare bulb to create strange misshapen shadows on the bare brick walls. In the centre of the room is a hulking something with a tarpaulin over it. Dunno how

I didn't trip over it when I came down. Davey's under the tarpaulin, and I call him to come out, but he won't budge. He's found an interesting scent down there and seems intent on sniffing all the flavour out of it. I don't want to leave without him, so I lift the corner of the tarp and reach for his collar.

Whatever's under there, it's metal and military green and has a tread on it like a tank. Is it a tank? No. It's big, but not that big. And how would she even get something like that down here? I let go of Davey's collar and he bounds back up the stairs, leaving me alone with the whatever it is.

I pull the tarp back a little more. Who's to say how far under I had to crawl to get Davey out? The explanation is already forming, on standby in case I need it later. There's one of the treads on each side, and they're roughly triangular, raising the body of the thing up high. The front is toughened glass, and on either side, there's huge jointed pneumatic rods, each with a fixture not a million miles away from the ones on Mrs Sutherland's arms. I stare at the thing for a long time, knowing what it is, but disbelieving.

"Can I have a go in it?" I look down and Lexi's beside me, twiddling her wand between her fingers.

"No," I say, quickly pulling the tarp back down, trying to make sure it looks exactly as I found it. "They're not toys. And don't you say nothing to Mrs S."

She rolls her eyes and skips back upstairs and I hurry after her but already she's yelling: "Mrs S, Mrs S, can I have a go in your mech?"

Mrs S is standing up when we get back. She's taller than expected, but it's hard to tell how much of that is just her legs. I thought she might be cross, but she just looks a little sad. She touches Lexi's shoulder and says: "Why don't we go take a closer look, huh?" And she gives me a long hard stare then, but I'm not sure what it means.

Mrs S clunks down the stairs, her legs hissing and buzzing with each step. She looks tired when we get to the bottom, like it takes more effort to lift those legs than you might think.

"So you lost your arms and legs in the war?" I say, wincing as soon as the words are out of my mouth. I'm as bad as Lexi.

"You could say that." She pulls the tarpaulin to the ground with a grand sweep. The mech is huge, frightening. Lexi doesn't seem to notice. She swings off one of the arms, pulls herself up into the cockpit as soon as Mrs S opens the hatch.

"How do I make it move? Can I fire the guns? Does it have rockets?"

Mrs Sutherland laughs. "No! You can't make it move because you don't have the interface implants. I was bomb disposal, so no rockets. And in any case, it was decommissioned years ago. You think they'd let me keep a weapon that can punch through a tank?"

"So why'd you bring it home?" asks Lexi, instantly bored.

I'm looking at that fist again, it's there, on the mech's paintwork, stencilled in black paint. A clenched fist with wings either side. And I know where I saw it. And I know why Mrs S don't have no arms or legs. And my stomach clenches as I imagine Dad in some military hospital, being carved up and fitted for his own mech to take to the front lines. A strangled sob bursts out of my mouth against my wishes and I pound back up the stairs, out of the front door, into the street. And I double over and look at the snow and it makes me dizzy the way the sun catches it and my tears melt little holes in the snow until I see spots everywhere and feel like I'm going to die.

"Sally!" Mrs Sutherland's calling from her doorway and I want to tell her everyone, absolutely everyone calls me Scally, but it isn't true because Dad doesn't and anyway my breath's still tearing through my chest, powering the sobs. Suddenly Davey has joined me outside and the snow makes him crazy. He runs in tight circles around me with his back humped up like a horseshoe and before I know it I'm laughing at him and forgetting—Forgetting that my Dad is probably—That when he gets home he'll be—I straighten my back, laughter gone, tears dried up, nothing left but me.

I look up at Mrs S and she holds her hand out to me. Lexi is at her side, peeping out round the floral old lady dress. Her little pudgy fingers grip Mrs S's other hand tight, like it ain't so bad to touch. I move forward, my own fingers outstretched towards that robot hand. If Lexi can do it, I can do it too, because the best thing about me, the absolute best thing, is I'm the oldest, bravest one.

Lynda Clark writes strange sci-fi, fantasy and horror. Two of her stories have received Honourable Mentions in the Writers of the Future Contest. Her work appears in the New Accelerator, Drabblecast and Beyond Science Fiction. Her short play about argumentative kitchen appliances won the BBC Award at the TCN Comedy WriterSlam. She's currently working on a PhD on interactive narrative, reader response and character agency. She can be found on Twitter complaining about videogames and television as @Notagoth

Don't Open Till Doomsday

.·

Mira

Benjamin Sperduto

The line started twitching again just after dawn.

Mira watched it closely as she heated up a pot of water to boil the rockbill eggs she scrounged up yesterday. By the time she dropped the first egg into the pot, the winch mechanism had creaked to life and slowly unspooled more line.

"He's descending again."

Parick stood near the edge of the sinkhole, his hand leaning against what remained of the sunken well.

"You'll beat him to the bottom if you don't keep away from there."

Mira dropped the second egg into the pot and stirred the water carefully. She hated rockbill eggs.

"Just thought you'd want to know." Parick moved away from the earthen maw and walked over to the winch. Firmly bolted onto the wagon, the device's hand-forged gears engaged in an ongoing tug of war over the slender rope coiled around its many spokes and spools. Inch by inch, more of the line fed down into the sinkhole nearby.

He reached for the cask of greased lard next to

the winch.

"Don't bother," Mira said. "I doused it before you got up."

She fished one of the eggs out of the pot. It smelled like rotten pigs' feet.

Parick sighed loudly as he joined her by the pot.

"Well what the hell am I supposed to be doing here, exactly?"

Mira tossed an egg to him.

"Eating."

He yelped when his hands closed around the still-hot shell.

"And keeping quiet."

She took the second egg out and smacked it against one of the stones ringing the campfire. The shell split, and a greenish gray puss seeped through the crack.

Parick grunted at the sight, but he wasn't close enough to smell it.

"Are you sure that's cooked enough?"
Mira shrugged as she pried the rest of the shell apart to reveal the soft, purple yolk inside.

"This is as done as they get. I'd eat it quick if I were you. Tastes twice as bad cold."

She popped the yolk into her mouth and swallowed it whole. Her throat tried to force the slimy thing back up, but she managed to choke it down to her stomach.

Parick groaned when he cracked his egg open and unleashed the stench inside. Mira considered letting him find out on his own how not to eat it, but she didn't care to deal with him retching all morning.

"Don't chew it," she said, "or else the taste will be in your mouth for hours. Just take a deep breath and gulp the whole thing down."

He tried to follow her advice, but gagged as soon as he swallowed. Mira fetched a wineskin and handed it to him.

"Drink."

A few gulps of liquid and a short coughing fit later, Parick meekly returned the wineskin.

"Disgusting."

Mira smiled. "Nothing tastes worse. At least nothing that won't make you sick. It'll keep your stomach busy for the rest of the day, though. Saves us a day or two of rations."

Parick grimaced and shook his head. "Not sure it's worth it."

The winch creaked to a halt.

"He stopped again," Parick said.

"Uh huh. And he'll probably start moving again in a few minutes whether you're staring at the line or not, so why don't you do something useful with that time instead? Get your horse saddled and go walk the perimeter."

Parick bit his lip as he glanced at the sunken well.

"What if he needs help or something? Shouldn't we—"

"I'm not paying you to mind the fucking line, Parick. Now get your ass on that horse and go check the perimeter."

He glared at her briefly before conceding with a sigh.

"Fine."

They'd fashioned a small, makeshift stable for Parick's horse inside a house some fifty yards from the sunken well. Aside from the crumbling, stone hovel near the well, it was the only structure in the abandoned village with an intact roof.

By the time Parick reached the house, the winch had ticked off a few more feet of line.

Mira tossed another log on the fire before she buttoned up her long coat. The wind had picked up a bit since sunrise, and the heavy cloud cover promised another cold, sunless day. After she cleaned and stowed the cooking pot and tongs, Mira retrieved her belt and lashed it over her coat, pulling it tight around her waist.

Parick led the horse back to the campsite before climbing up to the saddle.

"How far out should I check?" he asked.

"Half a mile's probably good. Close enough for me to hear a warning shot, anyway."

"Right. You seen the ox this morning?"

"Not yet," Mira said. "He usually doesn't wander too far, though."

Parick glanced at the winch. It had stopped again.

"Go on, then," Mira said. "You wouldn't know what to do with that thing anyway."

The horse grunted as Parick dug his heel into its flanks to urge it forward. Mira watched the beast trot down what used to be the main road leading through the village until it passed through the ruined gate and veered off to the west.

She walked over to the edge of the well and flicked the line with her finger. It held taut.

"Hit bottom yet?"

As if in response, the winch creaked quietly behind her, slowly unspooling more line inch by inch.

"Guess not."

Mira hoisted herself into the wagon and sat down next to the winch. After inspecting the device's various gears to make sure they were still rotating smoothly, she removed the wheellock pistol from her belt's holster and checked it for signs of rust. Once she was satisfied that the weapon was in good condition and that the gunpowder in the firing pan was still dry, she returned it to its holster and drew her rapier from its sheath to examine the blade for signs of wear.

She repeated the inspection ritual every half hour, each time convincing herself that she might have missed something. Occasionally, she hopped down from the wagon and examined the line feeding into the well. The rest of the time she spent scanning the village's ruined remains and wondering why the place had been abandoned. She eschewed the more likely explanations of war, famine, and disease in favor of fanciful explanations such as abduction by spirits from the nearby forest, a village-wide religious pilgrimage, or a spiritual rapture of one type or another.

Although she recognized the clear signs of death and desperation etched upon what remained of the village, she chose not to fill in the gaps between them. Some memories she preferred to leave undredged.

The winch stopped moving shortly after noon

and didn't start up again. Mira waited about an hour before she inspected the line. The length stretching from the winch to the well had more slack in it than before. She grabbed the line and shook it gently. It felt as loose as it looked.

A horse neighed loudly in the distance, and Mira's hand dropped to her wheellock.

Parick couldn't have completed his patrol already, she knew. After nearly a week in the village, she knew his routine almost as well as her own. The earliest she'd seen him return was three hours after noon on their first day, and after the scolding she gave him, he'd never returned that early again.

The sun remained muted behind the cloud cover, but she guessed that it couldn't have been more than two hours past midday.

Mira felt the familiar, cold tremor in her gut.

Something was wrong.

She drew the wheellock from its holster and cocked its firing pin into position.

"Don't be trying any of that, now."

The voice, coarse and slurred by a southerner's accent, came from her left. Mira glanced toward it to find a lone brigand standing next to a pile of stone and lumber some distance away from the well. Clad in a motley of hardened leathers and a few bits of steel, he trained a large pistol on her. The weapon had an unusually large barrel, so heavy that he had to steady it over his forearm.

It looked like a dragon gun of some kind.

"Put it down, pretty," he said. "Wouldn't want you to hurt yourself."

Mira counted off the distance between them.

Twenty, maybe twenty-five yards.

She looked the brigand over again. His coat was smeared with mud and tattered at the edges. He'd probably been sleeping in ditches for at least a month. Dragon guns could be pretty squirrely after a few weeks in the weather, especially if they lacked the proper powder and shot.

Mira took a deep breath.

"Last chance, bitch. Drop it now!"

She turned and ran toward the wagon. After her third step, she heard a loud cracking sound, followed by a thunderous boom. She dove to the ground as a few scattered projectiles harmlessly struck her coat or ricocheted off the cold soil. After rolling to her feet, Mira swung her wheellock's barrel toward the bewildered brigand, took aim, and fired.

The bullet sailed a bit off the mark, striking him at the base of the neck rather than piercing his heart. He staggered back against the crumbling wall, and dropped his dragon gun to clutch frantically at the bloody wound.

Mira ran for the wagon, wondering how many friends her ambusher had skulking about. Her answer came quickly as another bandit, this one a woman armed with a hatchet, leapt out from her hiding place near the wagon. Mira holstered her pistol and unsheathed her rapier before the woman could close the distance between them. The brigand lunged at her wildly as if she hoped to lop her head from her neck with a single blow. Mira ducked and counterattacked with two quick strikes, the first severing the tendons at the wrist and the second slicing across the back of the bandit's knee to send her tumbling to the ground.

"That'll be enough of that, dearie!"

Mira looked up to find two more brigands, a man and a woman, standing near the well. The woman, lean and wolf-faced, aimed a musket at her.

"I don't mean to go giving another warning. Drop that blade and lie down, now."

"Shit," Mira said, muttering through clenched teeth. She tossed her rapier aside and did the same with the wheellock. Then she knelt down to press her face against the ground.

"There's a good girl. Salis, get her tied up."

Rough hands pulled Mira's arms behind her back and bound them tightly. The wounded brigand nearby called out to her companions for help.

"How bad?" the woman asked. "Can she walk? Hold a sword?"

"Doubt it, Lyssa."

"Then put her down."

The wounded woman managed to cry out before a heavy, crunching blow silenced her.

Salis pulled Mira up and dragged her over to the campsite. By the time he got her there, a third brigand joined them, a ragged looking girl guiding a saddled horse.

Parick's horse.

"Ought to shoot that fucking thing," Salis said, gathering up Mira's weapons and tossing them down next to the campfire. "Damn near got all of us killed."

The girl with the horse only glared at her feet, though her left eye was so swollen that she probably couldn't see much out of it.

"Leave her be," Lyssa said. "Make yourself useful and go check on Nagy."

The brigand snorted and kicked dirt at the horse before trudging off towards the brigand Mira shot.

"Quite the fighter, ain't you, dearie?" Lyssa said.

The wolf-faced woman wore a dirty, bloodstained buff coat riddled with bullet holes underneath her moth-eaten riding cloak. Mira guessed that she'd scavenged them from the same dead cavalry officer that provided her knee-high leather boots. One of her eyes looked crooked, like her eye socket had been broken at some point and hadn't healed quite right.

"Hope you ain't caused more trouble than it's worth."

Lyssa ordered the girl to tie up the horse and rummage through the food and supplies around the encampment. By the time she got started, Salis had reached the body.

"Bled out," he said. "Bitch put a bullet through his neck."

Lyssa sat down across from Mira and sighed.

"Get his shit, then. He ain't going to be needing it where he's going."

The girl handed Lyssa a strip of jerky. She ate half of it before looking at Mira.

"Not many folks run when you point a dragon at them," she said as she chewed.

"Figured it was in as bad a shape as he was. Dragon barrels wear out pretty quick, especially if you don't have proper shot. What's he been using? Gravel? Woodchips?"

Lyssa chuckled as she swallowed.

"Dumb bastard's been scooping pebbles off the road since we left Dristbane. Said he was gonna add bits of bone from everybody he shot to the mix."

Mira hadn't been to Dristbane in years, but she knew it was about a week's ride to the west. Last she heard, the Duke of Barbathe was recruiting mercenaries to capture the city. That news was a few months old, though, and hearsay at that.

"Dristbane," Mira said, almost to herself. "Barbathe still have eyes on it?"

Lyssa sneered and spat at Mira's feet.

"He would if he still had them. Hired enough swords to do it and the city sued for terms when he showed up. Trouble was, they sent a hexer to negotiate. Captains looked in on them after an hour and found Barbathe hung by his guts with his skin inside out. Even nipped his cock and stuck it in his mouth just to tell him what they thought of his terms. Barbathe's brother didn't have the stones to stand and fight; slipped off with his banners that night without paying anyone. City attacked the camps at dawn, scattered what was left."

Mira could imagine what happened next. Stranded far from home without a battle to fight or any hope of getting paid, most of the mercenaries likely turned to raiding, plundering the area surrounding the city until somebody hired them away or put them down.

"How long since then?"

Lyssa glared at her for a moment before she shook her head and answered.

"That don't matter none to you, dearie. Don't go thinking that you can talk your way out of this."

Mira could have told her that she held no such delusions, but she kept her mouth shut.

Lyssa handed her musket to Salis before she pointed at the winch.

"Get up there and keep a sharp eye." She looked back to Mira. "You know how to work that thing?"

"Of course."

"How many you got down that hole?"

"Just one."

"Bullshit."

Lyssa reached down to her belt and drew a dagger from its sheath. The blade looked like it hadn't been wiped clean in years. She turned it over in her hand several times before looking back at Mira.

"Now I'm going to ask you again, dearie. How many men you got down there?"

"Just one," Mira said. "One delver, one winch, one line."

"One in the hole and one on top, eh? No other friends snooping around here anywhere?"

Mira glanced at Parick's horse.

"No."

Salis climbed onto the wagon and inspected the spools of rope wrapped around the gears and pullies as well as the various locking mechanisms that kept the winch in place.

"Wouldn't go messing with that if I was you," Mira said.

Lyssa jumped up and struck her with the back of her fist. The blow knocked Mira to the ground and split her lip. She tasted the blood trickling into her mouth. Lyssa grabbed her by her hair, pulled her head back, and pressed the dagger against her throat.

"I must have missed something, have I? Did somebody ask you a fucking question?"

Unable to shake her head and near gagging on her own spit, Mira choked out a garbled response, hoping that the brigand would interpret it correctly. Lyssa pressed the blade harder against her skin, and Mira clenched her teeth so tightly that she thought they might crack. Finally, the pressure relented. Lyssa removed the knife and whispered into her ear.

"Now then, who's in charge here, dearie?"

Mira swallowed, her saliva thickened with blood. "You are."

"One word from me and Salis will be getting his wish to fuck you bloody while we all watch, so you keep that in mind next time you've got a notion to open that pretty mouth of yours, got it?"

Mira nodded as she watched the filth-encrusted brigand rummaging through her wagon.

Lyssa pulled her off the ground and set her up on her knees.

The girl had gone to tend to the horse, but she kept stealing glances at Mira every so often. She couldn't have been more than fifteen.

Lyssa went back to twirling her knife. "How long has your delver been down there?" she asked.

"Near on a week."

"He hit bottom yet?"

"Maybe. Line's been still for a while."

Lyssa yanked Mira to her feet.

"Haul him up, then, and let's have a see what's he's got for us."

Mira shook her head. "I can't bring the line up yet."

Lyssa smiled, her jagged teeth glistening with saliva. "You can't? Or you won't?"

"He won't hook anything he finds to the line until he's ready to come up."

Salis groaned.

"Fuck sake. This ain't worth the risk. How long you plan to sit around waiting for this to pay out?"

"Shut up, Salis," Lyssa said. "There's a good reason you ain't the one doing the thinking around here." She turned to the girl. "Find anything to drink?

The girl offered Lyssa one of the wineskins tucked under the bag of jerky. She gulped down about a third of it in one swig.

"Not bad. Better than nothing leastways." She wiped the corner of her mouth with her coat sleeve. "Ain't had a decent drink since we left Tarrow."

Mira gave her room enough to talk if she wanted. Sellswords and common soldiers didn't often care for silence. It sounded too much like death.

Lyssa tossed the wineskin aside and sighed. "Should've wintered there. Garrison pay was shit, but it would've been enough to see us through to spring. Fighting might shift by then, take us somewhere warmer than this witch's cunt of a country."

Tarrow was three weeks to the south, a difficult ride across war-ravaged country. The city of Iothic used to split the distance between Tarrow and Dristbane. Mira wintered there once when she was younger, maybe as young as the brigand girl with the horse. Rumor had it that scavengers and refugees now squatted amidst what remained of the place.

"What's the nearest town from here?"

"Madroc. Forty miles north."

Lyssa rubbed her forehead. "Long way to walk this time of year."

Mira didn't like the way Lyssa stared at the wagon. There would be plenty of room there for the three brigands if they cut the winch loose. If Lyssa got it in her head that they were better off making for Madroc without waiting for the line to come up, Mira had a feeling they wouldn't want to bother hauling a prisoner along.

Something moved near the lip of the sinkhole. She glanced over and saw a white rat running along the line toward the winch.

Lyssa saw it too.

"That your delver's signal?"

Mira nodded.

"Salis, get that thing running."

"Wait," Mira said. "Let me do it. He's liable to strip out the gears"

Lyssa glared at her, then pulled her up and cut her bonds.

"Keep a close eye on her, Salis."

The brigand trained his musket on Mira as she approached.

Mira locked the winch's gears into position and turned the crank to begin reeling in the line. The first few revolutions were hard, but once the winding mechanism got underway, the work became much easier. Within a few minutes, the line coiled around the spool quickly, eating up several yards with every turn of the crank.

When Lyssa went to peer into the sinkhole, Mira saw her chance.

She eased off on the crank, acting as if it had grown difficult to turn.

"Gears are getting dry," she said to Salis. "Grab some lard from that cask and wipe it on the gears, will you?"

Grumbling, the brigand set his musket down and scooped up a fistful of lard.

"Right there," Mira said, nodding at the array of interlocking, exposed gears.

When Salis leaned toward the winch, she reached over, shoved him forward, and let go of the crank.

The spinning gears caught his sleeve and pulled him into the gears up to his elbow, his bones crunching loudly beneath the metal teeth. He screamed and tried to pull away, but Mira smashed his face against the winch's metal frame and snatched up his musket. She slammed the musket's butt against the back of his skull, cracking it like an overripe rockbill egg.

Dealing with Salis cost her precious seconds, enough time for Lyssa to react to her betrayal. She lunged at Mira and hauled her out of the wagon, sending the musket flying through the air. They crashed to the ground in a tangle of limbs.

Mira tried to roll away and locate the musket, but Lyssa caught her by the hair before she could get clear.

"You bitch!"

Mira remembered Lyssa's wretched knife as the brigand yanked her head back. She clenched her teeth, expecting to feel the dull blade sawing into her windpipe any moment.

Instead, she heard a gunshot.

Lyssa cried out and let go of her hair. Mira rolled away and got to her knees. She found the wolf-faced woman lying face down on the ground, gasping wetly for air. Each breath brought up a bit of blood and her limbs twitched haphazardly. A fresh splotch of blood in the center of her back grew steadily larger with each breath, and her limbs twitched haphazardly. Shattered spine. Probably a punctured lung as well.

Bad way to go.

The girl stood a short distance beyond the wounded brigand, smoking musket in hand. She stared at Lyssa for a few seconds before she dropped the weapon and sat down next to the campfire.

Mira joined the girl after she caught her breath. She looked like she was sobbing, but didn't make a sound while she did it.

That kind of crying took practice.

"What's your name, girl?"

It took her a while to answer.

"E... Eaven," she said, her voice trembling.

Gently, Mira placed her hand on the girl's shoulder. She flinched, but didn't pull away completely.

"Did they hurt you?"

Eaven nodded.

"How long?"

"Tarrow. Since Tarrow."

Mira could have pressed her for details, but she knew they didn't really matter. It made no difference why she left Tarrow in such ill company, only that she wouldn't have to keep it any longer.

"We'll be heading to Modroc once my delver gets topside. If you want to leave now, I won't stop you, but it'd be wiser if you stick with us till then."

The girl wouldn't look at her, but she nodded.

"My name's Mirasel," she said. "But you can call me Mira."

A few yards away, Lyssa managed to flop over onto her back. Her breathing sounded thicker, like she'd swallowed a glob of cold honey.

Eaven glanced back at her. For a moment, her bruised face betrayed a hint of pity.

"Should we..."

Mira grunted.

"Fuck her. Let the bitch bleed."

Eaven, looking a little relieved, nodded.

"Come help me pull that other bastard out of the gears," Mira said. "If we're lucky, we've got a payday on the other end of that line."

It took them the better part of an hour to clear what remained of Salis from the machinery. They dumped it behind one of the old houses along with Lyssa's corpse. After they finished, Mira once again locked the gears into position and turned the winch's crank to haul up the line.

Corver finally emerged from the sinkhole just

after midday. Mira helped him over the ledge and unbuckled the hooks that secured him to the line. A layer of dirt and soot covered most of his body.

"Well?" Mira asked. "Don't keep us in suspense. What'd you find?"

He grunted. "Nice to see you too, love of my life."

Mira hated being called that. Many things described their marriage, but love was not one of them. She glared at him until he stopped grinning.

"Maybe scrounged up enough to keep us going for a bit," Corver said. "Nothing we can retire on, though."

Mira went back to turning the crank. The large sacks tied to the end of the line emerged next. Corver stacked them with the rest of their supplies.

"Odds and ends, mostly," he said. "We weren't the first that's been here. Most of the good stuff got picked clean, probably a few years back from the looks of it."

Corver finally noticed Eaven tending to the campfire when he sat down to dust off his clothing.

"Who the hell's this?"

"Name's Eaven," Mira said. "Family's been dead a while. Told her she could ride with us far as Modroc."

Corver shrugged.

"Whatever. Where's Parick?"

"Haven't seen him since this morning. Horse came back without him."

"Could be a bad sign," he said. "We'd best get moving. You need a hand with that crank?"

"No, I'm fine."

"Suit yourself. Anything exciting happen while I was gone?"

Mira shook her head. "Nothing I couldn't manage."

.·˙

Benjamin Sperduto is a history teacher and has also worked as a freelance editor and writer for roleplaying games. His short stories have appeared in a number of anthologies, including Coven (Purple Sun Press), Bad Neighborhood (Spooky Words Press), and Dystopian Express (Hydra Publications). His first novel, The Walls of Dalgorod, is available from Curiosity Quills Press. A graduate of the University of South Florida, he lives and works in Tampa, Florida. For a full list of publications and fiction updates, visit www.benjaminsperduto.com or follow him on Twitter (@bensperduto).

Don't Open Till Doomsday

Planet of the Neanderthals

Melissa Ferguson

Ginger was the only Neo-Neanderthal in the waiting room of the face sculpting clinic. Two men sat across from her, their faces slack, lost in some entertainment on their MindComm brain implants.

Ginger's Sapien mother placed her hand on an OmniScreen on the wall.

"Welcome Tabitha Nestle," the Clinic Intelligence System said, "Please take a seat. You'll be called when a consultation booth becomes available."

"Thank you." Mum sat, patted Ginger on the thigh and turned inward to her MindComm.

Ginger jiggled her knee. The walls, floors, ceiling and chairs were all varying shades of white. She studied the perfect faces of the two men across from her. Unlike Sapiens, Neos had no MindComms to distract and entertain them.

After several tedious minutes they were called. Mum jostled her into the consultation booth. A large upright cylinder closed around her and a mirror slid down until Ginger could see her pale reflection. Beads of sweat formed on her forehead. There wasn't enough air in the cylinder. She breathed deeply. The net-brochure had claimed the scan was non-invasive and painless, but it hadn't mentioned she'd be imprisoned in an airless booth while it happened.

"Neo-Neanderthal Clone number 6154-CH detected. Sixteen years of age. Female. Designated adopted child. Property of Tabitha Nestle," the Clinic Intelligence System said. "I will now read a list of procedures available to Neo-Neanderthals: Sapienization, Scar Removal, Skin Re-shading, Other. Please state clearly the quotation you require."

"Sapienization."

"Sapienization quotation requested. Preparing for scan now." The inner workings of the machine whirred and hummed. "Close your eyes... Stand as still as possible... Breathe in deeply ... and hold. Scanning now."

Bright purple light pierced Ginger's eyelids and a soft high-pitched whine filled her ears. Her lungs burned.

"Scan complete. You may breathe and open your eyes." The sides of the cylinder swung open and Ginger gasped a lungful of air. "Thank you, Clone 6154-CH. The quotation has been sent to Tabitha Nestle. We hope you choose Paragon Face Sculpting to create the best possible you. Have a lovely day."

Outside the clinic Mum placed her palm on the biometric panel of a parking rack. A self-driving solar car disengaged and unfolded. They climbed inside and joined the stream of cars and cyclists.

"It's a little more expensive than I expected, but they are the best face-sculpting clinic in the city. I was browsing through their before and after pictures in the waiting room. We could look like sisters." Mum's youth-preserved face lit-up. "They'll make your nose smaller, put in a bit of a chin, file down the bone on that brow. Tooth replacement is a bit out of our budget at the moment." Mum's hands flew around Ginger's face from one unsatisfactory feature to another.

Ginger cringed and pressed herself back into her seat. Life would be easier the more Sapien-like she became. But being Sapien-like required vigilant removal of excess body hair; minimal exercise to keep muscle bulk down; hair-styles that disguised a watermelon-shaped head; and clothing to conceal short limbs, big knee-caps and a barrel chest. Neos who'd been Sapienized didn't look like Neos anymore, but they didn't really look like Sapiens either. They became some third variety of human, trapped behind immobile, clay-like faces.

"I've sent an inquiry about payment plans. There are a few other clinics whose rates might be a bit more reasonable. We'll get more quotes before we decide."

"Do you think the surgery will hurt, Mum?"

"No pain, no gain, sweetie. It'll all be worth it in the end."

Ginger crossed her arms over her chest. What was so bad about being a Neanderthal anyway? Her species had prevailed for hundreds of thousands of years and had been thought special enough to be reincarnated from scraps of DNA found in ancient bones.

Ginger's family apartment was in one of the hundreds of buildings in the highrise forest of the city. Holograms and digi-screens of Neanderthal skeletons and famous Neo-Neanderthal entertainers and athletes adorned her bedroom walls. Colourful fabrics and cushions, purchased from second-hand shops in the industrial quarter of the city, covered her bed. The rest of the house was a uniform grey, furnished with nano-assembled and 3D printed goods. Mum and Dad's MindComms overlaid the utilitarian blandness with a pleasant augmented reality of their choice.

Ginger picked up her OmniScreen and sent a message to her Neo friend, Garnet.

Garnet replied immediately. *Face Sculpting!? How barbaric! I'll talk to Dad about it tonight. See you at school tomorrow. Hugs. Garnet.* Garnet's adoptive father was a doctor.

Thoughts of the surgery and its consequences whirled in her mind. At least at home she had a source of distraction.

"AIS."

"Yes, Ginger," the Apartment Intelligence System answered.

"Keeping Up With The Cavemen on TeevScreen please."

On the reality show—which featured a Neo-Neanderthal group living in the wild—survival experts were reacquainting the Neos with their instincts. The men chased rabbits with stabbing spears and the women collected edible weeds and plants. Ginger tutted and picked up her OmniScreen.

They obviously know nothing about Neanderthals, Ginger posted on The Pleistocene People's Forum. *There was no division of labour in Neanderthal groups. Men and women hunted together.*

Ginger gave a quiet cheer as one of the characters on-screen speared a rabbit.

Ginger slung her school bag over her shoulder and walked along the solar-panelled footpath. Passengers in self-driving cars yelled at the cyclists streaming around them and setting off their proximity sensors. Advertising and delivery drones buzzed overhead, negotiating the spaces between buildings with the control and dexterity of insects. The lingering smell of the anti-biological wash, which bathed the city streets every night, tickled Ginger's nose.

She pressed a button beside the glass entry doors of the building hosting her school.

"How may I help you?" the Building Intelligence System said.

"Neo-Neanderthal Vocational Training. Level twenty-one."

"Please present your clone tattoo to the sensor above the door."

Ginger turned and angled the back of her neck toward the sensor.

"Thank you, clone 6154-CH. You may enter." The glass doors slid open. "Enjoy your lessons."

"Thank you, BIS."

Ginger waited in the foyer until Garnet arrived. Garnet gave her a hug and they walked over to the elevator.

"I spoke to Dad about Sapienization." Garnet shook her head. "It's a really awful procedure. He's seen Neos in chronic pain afterwards. And without Medi-Implants some have died of superbug infections. What are your parents thinking?"

Ginger blinked back tears. The elevator arrived.

"Floor twenty-one, please," Garnet said to BIS.

Ginger considered her reflection in the mirrors lining the elevator walls.

"My parents don't love me. Do they?"

Garnet gave Ginger a kiss on the cheek and squeezed her arm.

"I've always suspected it, but I'd hoped that one day they'd do something to prove me wrong. You know?"

Garnet nodded and bit her lip.

"It's probably my fault."

"How could it be your fault? You're a lovely, sweet person."

"Maybe my time in The LINC destroyed my ability to connect with people." Ginger's only memories of her first three years spent in The Levallois Institute for Neanderthal Cloning were no more than fragments and snapshots; figures in biohazard suits, shiny white walls, fluorescent lighting, metal-barred cots and twirling her fingers in another toddlers reddish-brown hair.

"It's not you, Ginger. You connect with people just fine."

The elevator doors opened and they walked to their classroom.

At nine AM their teacher projected his consciousness into an android at the front of the class. "Good morning students." The android powered up the TeevScreen and launched into a lesson on the proper handling of lab meat to prevent bacterial contamination.

Ginger tried to concentrate. It would be so much easier if Neos could get their education and career-packs downloaded to a MindComm like Sapien kids.

Garnet nudged her with her elbow and tilted her OmniScreen. *It's not worth it. You have to tell your parents "NO". Get them to talk to my Dad. Maybe he can make them see sense.*

Ginger nodded and turned back toward the TeevScreen. She knew Garnet was right, but how would she ever make Mum and Dad understand?

A robo-cleaner slid across the already spotless stainless steel surfaces of the kitchen. Mum sat, blank-faced, at the dining table.

"Mum." Ginger stood before her mother's unseeing eyes, pressing her hands to the butterflies in her stomach. "Mum…"

"AIS."

"Yes, Ginger?"

"Can you contact Mum on MindLine and let her know I want to talk to her?"

"Of course, Ginger."

Mum sighed and focussed on Ginger. "I'm

finishing up some work at the office, Ginger. What do you want?"

"It's about the face-sculpting appointment."

"We don't need to leave for another half-an-hour yet." Mum's face slackened again.

"Mum...Mum."

Mum raised an eyebrow. "What, Ginger?"

"I don't want to go."

"What do you mean? What's wrong?"

"I don't want to have the surgery. Garnet's dad says it's dangerous."

Mum stood and put her hands on her hips. "Your father and I have worked extra hours to earn the credits for this. I understand you're nervous, but it's happening. You'll be grateful once it's completed."

"But I'm scared—

Mum closed her eyes and held up her hand. "Enough. I don't have time for this. Be ready in half an hour."

Ginger ran to her bedroom, tears clouding her eyes. She slammed her bedroom door and grabbed her OmniScreen. She forwarded a message from Garnet's father, explaining the dangers of the Sapienization procedure, to her mother's MindMail. A moment later the OmniScreen pinged with a message.

Ginger, I will not enter into any more discussion on this matter. We're doing this for your own good. Sapienization will open up opportunities for you. I will see you at the solar-car rack in thirty minutes. Mum.

Ginger lay back on her bed. She supposed she'd been a disappointment. Her parents had adopted her after exhausting all the reproductive technologies available. Sapien cloning was illegal and for many childless couples a Neo child was the last resort.

She'd thought of running away before, but had always been too afraid. Runaway, discarded and unemployed Neos usually ended up as medical research test subjects. With an occupation she'd be entitled to a bed at the Neo workers barracks. Ginger turned to The Pleistocene People's Forum.

Leaving home. Need a job. Can anyone help?- Ginger-Haired Girl.

She packed some clothes into a bag and checked the forum. There were two public responses. One encouraging her to join the Security Force Reserves and the other from a club that employed Neo exotic dancers. In her private mailbox were two more messages. The first from a man who organised illegal Neo fights. Ginger deleted it and went on to the last message.

Hello Ginger-Haired Girl. I'm one of the casting agents for the reality TV show "Keeping Up With The Cavemen." We're casting another Neanderthal reality programme and think you'd be perfect. If you'd like to meet and hear more about this opportunity pm me. Cheers Ferdinand05.

Ginger stood beside the smooth metal of the ten-metre high city wall. Each time an armoured delivery truck came in or out of the nearby gate Ginger heard the roar of humanity on the other side. She shrank back, imagining slum dwellers rushing the gate like a tidal wave. Why did Ferdinand ask to meet her here, of all places?

A truck pulled into a parking bay and a large man, with shoulders even broader than Ginger's, got out. Bull horns protruded from his forehead; a transgene punk.

"Ginger?" The man walked toward her.

"Ferdinand?"

"Yes. A pleasure to meet you." He held out his hand and Ginger looked at it for a moment. There were heavy penalties for unsolicited physical contact with Sapiens. He grasped her hand and pumped it twice. "We best be on our way."

Ginger's mouth went dry. "What do you mean? Where are we going?"

Ferdinand peered left and right, leant toward Ginger and whispered, "Our headquarters are near the Keeping Up With The Cavemen secret location. We do all our business from there. If we have time you can have a peek at the cast."

"Oh."

Ginger hadn't been beyond the wall since she'd been adopted. The LINC was located several miles out of the city along with industrial complexes too large, dangerous or controversial to operate within the safety of the city wall. The only other people outside the city, besides the slum-dwellers, were anti-government and terrorist groups such as Transhumanists and Anti-Tekkers.

Ginger climbed into the truck and Ferdinand drove it to the gate. A Neo Security Force Officer held out an OmniScreen. Ferdinand placed his hand on it until it beeped.

"What's your business outside the city?"

"Delivering nano-disassembled waste to manufacturers."

Ginger looked at him and frowned. Ferdinand winked.

Another Neo Officer waved a scanner wand over Ginger's tattoo. She wondered if Mum and Dad had noticed she was missing and put an alert out. Part of her wished they had. The scanning wand gave a benign beep. Mum was probably zoned out on the couch after a dose of KalmWash from her brain implant.

"And you miss, what is your business?"

"She's on labouring work experience," Ferdinand said.

"Okay. Have a nice day." The Neo Officers stepped away from the truck and the metal gate slid back into the wall.

"Why did you tell them that?"

Ferdinand shook his head. "You're new to this. There are spies everywhere trying to learn the location of the set. It's worth a lot of credits to the paparazzi. If I told the guards they'd probably call it in for a reward and send a drone after us."

They entered the slums and Ginger's mouth fell open. In all directions were people of all shapes and sizes. Old people and ugly people too, not like in the city where no one appeared a day over thirty and everyone was beautiful and perfect. Children ran barefoot around the truck, throwing rocks. People huddled under flaps of material and in makeshift dwellings. The smoke from cooking fires and the stench of open-pit toilets filled the cab. A man waved a gun and yelled something unintelligible. Ferdinand pressed a button and the windows began to roll closed.

The man with the gun clambered onto the truck's running board. His grey skin and bulging eyes only inches from Ginger. He spat at the gap in the closing window and Ginger flinched. The man cackled and jump back to the ground.

"Don't worry. It would take a nuclear bomb to penetrate this truck," Ferdinand said.

Ginger wiped flecks of spittle from her face.

A long line of slum-dwellers snaked away from the door of a large GovCorp caravan. Neo and Android Security Force Officers surrounded the van. Ginger remembered news reports about the riots and obstruction of trade routes that had led to the rollout of MindComms and Medi-Implants to the slummies.

After twenty minutes the slums gave way to the remnants of the suburbs. Ginger had read that people used to live in single or sometimes double-storey, stand-alone houses, spread out from the city, but able to commute easily due to the abundance of fossil fuels. Now the homes of these Sapiens of the past were crumbling piles of rubble. Plants had broken through the thin crust of concrete imprisoning them and invaded the houses; simultaneously tearing down and reinforcing the structures.

After a while the carcasses of the houses thinned and they entered the industrial zone. All the complexes shrouded by high, razor-wired fences.

Night had fallen by the time Ferdinand turned off the highway onto an unlit, unsealed road. The truck headlights bounced off head high grass and weeds. A dilapidated weatherboard house, surrounded by rusted car skeletons, rose out of the undergrowth. Light spilled from the windows.

"This is your headquarters?" Ginger had imagined something more professional, well lit and surrounded by a chain link fence and Security Force Officers.

"It's a work in progress. We're about to begin renovations."

Inside wallpaper hung from the walls like streamers and the house smelt dusty and mouldy. The floorboards were buckled and faded. A tall woman took Ginger by the shoulders and kissed her on both cheeks.

"Welcome, I'm Peony. You must be Ginger."

Ginger nodded, words stuck in her throat. This wasn't at all like she'd expected.

Peony ushered Ginger over to an old couch with a faded rose pattern, stuffing burst from tears in the fabric. "I think you'll be just perfect for our new show." She waved her hands around. "Sorry about the state of this place. Did Ferdinand explain we're starting renovations soon?" She didn't wait for Ginger's answer. "Make yourself comfortable. I'll bring you a drink."

Ginger rolled a piece of couch-stuffing between her fingers. She supposed it made sense. Everything outside the city walls was bound to need renovation.

Peony and Ferdinand spoke in low voices in the adjoining kitchen. Something scuttled in a dark corner. Peony returned with a glass of cola. Mum had never allowed Ginger to have sweetened drinks, she'd said that without the MetaBoost function provided by a

Medi-Implant they'd make her fat. The cola sparkled in the light. Tiny bubbles raced to the surface and popped. She took a sip. She'd never tasted anything so sweet. The bubbles burnt her throat and fizzed in her empty belly.

"Now, Ferdinand and I will get the camera ready for your screen test. You finish your drink and then we'll start. Just a formality, of course. I can tell already you're going to be perfect." Peony followed Ferdinand out of the room.

Ginger took another sip. The sweetness and fizz were unpleasant and there was a slightly bitter aftertaste. What a disappointment. She looked around for somewhere to empty her glass. Tattered curtains blew in and out of one of the windows. Ginger tip-toed over and poured the cola into the dirt.

She concentrated on her breathing and tried to calm her thumping heart. She'd been such a fool coming all this way out of the safety of the city with a complete stranger just because he claimed he'd put her on television. Such a naïve Neanderthal thing to do. No wonder Sapiens had superseded them all those years before.

Ginger's breathing calmed and her heartbeat slowed. She yawned. Sugar furred her teeth. She ran her tongue around her mouth. Something was wrong, but her mind struggled to grasp it. Her eyes drooped. She forced them open and shook her head. This wasn't the time to sleep. Maybe if she walked around she would wake-up. Her limbs were too heavy to lift. She closed her eyes for a moment, just to give them a rest.

A Security Force Officer with a scalpel chased

her. He wanted to cut out her bones and put them in a museum. He caught her and sliced a horizontal line on the back of her neck. She swam through the murky depths of sleep back into consciousness and opened her eyes to peeling linoleum floor tiles. The back of her neck stung, right where her clone tattoo was. She screamed and scrambled to sit up.

"She's awake!" Ferdinand yelled.

Ginger was lying on the kitchen table. She got to her knees and clapped a hand over the back of her neck.

"That's impossible. I put two tabs in her drink. They never wake up if they've had two."

Ferdinand and Peony stood on opposite sides of the table, eyes wide. A scalpel dangled from Peony's fingers.

"Oh no, oh no, oh no. Please don't hurt me. I won't tell anyone. Just let me go."

Ferdinand glanced at Peony. "We were just removing your tattoo. It's a perk of working with us. You can't be traced or detected."

Peony nodded. "That's right and of course we didn't want to cause you any pain or distress. Why don't I give you something for the pain and then we can finish the procedure?"

The kitchen cabinet doors were cracked and hanging off their hinges. Cobwebs fell from the roof like stalactites. Ginger shook her head and tears welled in her eyes.

"No, you're lying. The Cavemen cast all have tattoos. What do you want with me?"

Peony and Ferdinand exchanged another

glance.

"Just calm down and I'll tell you the truth." Peony put the scalpel down.

The truth. Ginger wanted the truth to be that she really was going to be a famous Neo entertainment star and that she hadn't been drugged and lied to and she wasn't about to have her organs harvested, or be raped and killed, or whatever these people wanted with her. She whimpered.

"We're a Neo rights group. We're removing your tattoo so you can't be traced. We'll take you to a safe house with other Neos who've escaped GovCorp."

Ferdinand nodded. "You'd like that wouldn't you?"

"No... I don't know. I just want to go home. Please let me go." Ginger hugged herself to contain her shaking.

"Calm down and think about what we're saying. This is a great opportunity for you," Ferdinand said.

"Let me make you a cup of tea and we can talk about it." Peony held her hands toward Ginger.

"I...I just want to go."

"Okay..." Ferdinand grimaced. "We won't force you to do anything you don't want to do, but it's a long way back to the city and dangerous through the slums. Let me call a friend of mine who might be heading there tonight." Ferdinand's face went blank as he engaged with his MindComm.

Ginger slid off the table. "No. Don't call anyone." She ran towards the kitchen door.

Peony stood in her way and reached for her. "Please, Ginger—"

Ginger pushed Peony and she slammed against the wall.

"Hey," Ferdinand said and seized Ginger's shoulder.

An image from a Neo fight flashed into her mind. She clutched Ferdinand's face and head-butted him with her powerful brow ridge. Bones cracked and blood spurted from his nose. He collapsed onto the ground holding his face. Peony shrieked and cowered on the floor. Ginger grabbed her bag from the lounge, and burst out of the front door.

Adrenaline and moonlight guided her down the dark track and away from the house. She hugged her bag to her chest and looked over her shoulder every few metres. No one gave chase. At the main road she took cover from the passing trucks in the tangle of vegetation at the side of the road. The grass and weeds grabbed at her, hundreds of tiny hands trying to hold her back.

The cut on the back of her neck throbbed, but it was only superficial. She could endure pain. The skeletons of her ancestors documented multiple traumas they'd lived through.

She searched through her bag for her OmniScreen, planning to contact her parents. How pathetic; her independence had lasted less than twenty-four hours. The OmiScreen was gone. She'd become a cautionary tale of Neo stupidity.

Further down the road a sphere of light rallied against the darkness; a fuelling station. Squinting against the fluorescent lights, she walked past the fuel pumps and electric chargers to the store. A sign on the sliding doors, Sapien Citizens Only, stopped her.

Two Neo Security Force Officers manned the entrance. Ginger opened her mouth to speak. One of the guards shook his head, pushed her gently aside with his stunner and glanced up at a security camera. She gave a small nod to indicate she understood. Maybe somewhere, in a parallel universe, there was a planet where Neanderthals emerged from pre-history to become the dominant human species and Sapiens had faded away. A planet where Neanderthals were treated like people.

Her stomach rumbled and her legs were weak and rubbery. The last thing she'd eaten was porridge for breakfast.

An armoured delivery truck lit her in its headlights. She hurried out of the way.

"Hey," a man's voice called behind her. She kept walking, assuming he was talking to someone else.

"Hey, Neo girl."

Ginger turned. There was nowhere to run to. The truck driver—a young Sapien male—walked toward her, his hands in the air.

"Sorry. I didn't mean to frighten you. I've never seen a Neo alone out here. I thought you might need some help." He stood a couple of metres away. "Are you okay? Can I contact someone for you? I know these places have a really shitty anti-Neo policy."

Ginger bit her lip. Could she trust him? She had nowhere to go and she was terrified of passing through the slums alone and unguarded. And what if Peony and

Ferdinand came after her with reinforcements or weapons?

"Maybe you could contact my mum for me."

The driver smiled. "Sure. Glad to be of help."

Ginger gave him her mother's MindLine ID and told him her own name. He focussed inward. How would she know he was talking to her mum and not calling Ferdinand to come and get her? Ginger studied his face for some tell-tale sign of honesty or deception.

After several minutes he disengaged. "Tabitha's worried to death about you. She's sure she's suffered some unnecessary cellular ageing in the last twelve hours."

He'd definitely been talking to her mum.

"Is she coming to get me?"

"She doesn't have transportation beyond the city walls. I told her I'm on my way back to the city and she's happy for you to ride with me. But you're not to wake her when you get in because she has an important meeting tomorrow."

Ginger rolled her eyes.

"Oh and she said something about the face-sculpting issue would need to be revisited too." The driver screwed up his nose. "She sounds quite...um... formidable."

"That's Mum."

The driver smiled. "My name's Todd."

While Todd refuelled Ginger waited in the truck. He brought back a soy mince pie and a nutrient water for her.

"You looked hungry."

Ginger held the warm pie in her hands. "Thank you."

They drove along in silence for a while. The night sky was much darker and the stars much brighter without the corruption of the city lights.

Todd cleared his throat. "Do you mind me asking how you got out here?"

The story tumbled out of Ginger.

Todd shook his head. "You were wise to run. Most likely they were organ harvesters."

The truck's entertainment panel lit up and the familiar tune that preceded GovCorp community service announcements played.

Good evening citizens. The roll-out of MindComms and Medi-Implants to non-citizen Sapiens, has been completed. A software update to synchronize all implants will occur in three days, on the 17th of this month. Thank you for your attention. GovCorp will now return you to your selected entertainment.

Just before midnight Todd dropped her off at her building. She crept through the still, dark apartment and fell asleep fully-clothed on top of her bed.

Ginger awoke the next day with a sore throat. She drank a nutri-shake and stepped into the shower. Hot water ran across the back of her neck, stiff and sore where Peony had cut her. White spots swarmed before her eyes and the world spun. She placed her hand on the shower wall and crouched. Every muscle in her body wanted to dissolve into a puddle and slide down the drain. She turned off the water and stumbled back to bed.

Ginger moved in and out of consciousness. Her waking moments alternated between drowning in a layer of burning hot sweat and shivering as though immersed in a bathtub of ice.

She awoke to two paramedics loading her onto a stretcher. She ached; her lips were cracked and bleeding and her head pounded. She tried to sit up.

"It's okay. We're taking you to the Neo-Neanderthal Health Centre," one of the paramedics said.

She relaxed back onto the stretcher. She must have picked up a virus that the Sapiens had a level of resistance to. Her own immune system had evolved before the agricultural revolution; prior to domesticated animals and life in high density conditions. She drifted back into unconsciousness.

She roused again. Noises and voices echoed around her. She couldn't move. Her body tingled numbly. Everything was blurred, like trying to see underwater. Her hearing came in and out. People bustled around. Machines beeped and hummed.

Ginger's thickened tongue stuck to the roof of her mouth. She blinked and tried to make the world come into focus. Colours swirled above Ginger, like oil on water. A high-pitched buzz filled her ears and the world disappeared again.

***

Ginger awoke thirsty and aching. She opened her eyes. The light from the window sent a bolt of pain through her head. She squinted and pushed onto her elbows. Tubing in her arm led to a flat, empty plastic bag hanging from an iv pole. She pressed the buzzer for the nurse and stretched into her sore limbs. Not a sound came from the hallway or the street outside. She pulled the needle out of her arm and swung her legs over the side of the bed. The three other beds in the room were vacant; the covers flung back as though the occupants had left in a hurry.

"BIS?"

No response. She put her feet to the floor and pushed out of bed. Her muscles were putty and her legs wobbled. She leant against the wall as she moved.

The hallway outside her room was quiet and still.

"Hello. Nurse?"

She peered into the other rooms along the hallway—all devoid of life. A man sat at the nurse's station, his face on the desk.

"Hello," Ginger said.

The man didn't move. Ginger wrinkled her nose against a smell like bedpans and rotting meat.

"Nurse? HEY!" Her voice echoed through the building.

Ginger reached over and nudged his shoulder. His head fell sideways, exposing glassy red eyes and dried stripes of blood. A fly crawled out of his nose. Ginger screamed and scuttled backwards until her back was against the wall. She slid down and struggled to breathe.

Footsteps came from her left. The short stocky silhouette of a Neo male moved toward her. She froze. Had he killed the nurse? Did he mean to harm her?

The man came closer. A stained bandage was wound around his skull.

"You woke up okay then?" He stopped in front of her.

Ginger swallowed.

He squatted and peered into her eyes.

"What's going on here? Where is everyone? What happened to the nurse?"

He shook his head. "I'm not really sure myself. I woke yesterday and it was all like this." He waved his hand in the air. "Most of the Sapiens are dead. None of us Neos though. All the other Neos left, but I thought I ought to stay in case you woke."

"What happened to the Sapiens?"

"Don't know for sure. Maybe some virus that Neos are immune to. Maybe something to do with their brain implant update. I suppose we'll find out sooner or later." He shrugged. "Maybe we'll never know."

"What do we do now? There must be someone to report to. Neo Control or—"

"There's no one left to report to."

Ginger choked back a sob. Mum, Dad, even that nice truck driver, Todd, would all be dead.

The man squeezed her shoulder. "Cheer up. Look at it this way—it's our turn." He stood up and spread his arms out. "Fuck you evolution. It's planet of the Neanderthals now."

Melissa Ferguson is a mother of two, cancer-fighting scientist and defender of the reputation of Neanderthals. While her family sleeps she thinks about cyborgs, cults, zombies, enchanted woods, future science, demons, extinct species of humans, evil scientists and infectious diseases, and tries to mash them together into awesome stories. Melissa is currently working on futuristic, post-apocalyptic novel set in the world of Planet of the Neanderthals. Her short stories have appeared in Postscripts to Darkness, Pavor Nocturnis Dark Fiction Anthology, [untitled], and Island. She has a neglected writing blog at melissajaneferguson.com

The Comeback

Ross Baxter

Stella stopped outside the brightly painted door of the Managing Director of EK Records and paused a moment; as Ed Kane's Personal Assistant she had been involved in lots of weird stuff in the last five years, but nothing as weird as this. She took a deep breath, knocked loudly, and then pushed open the door.

"The Russian's have just called, Mr Kane," she announced curtly. "They've finally done it."

Kane looked up from his X-Box, his face blank whilst he processed what she had told him. Then he suddenly understood and a look of absolute delight spread across his wrinkled face.

"Finally!" he yelled, punching the air. "When can I talk to him?"

Stella sighed inwardly; although Kane had been taken through this many times he still did not seem to be able to comprehend what he was paying a vast amount of money for. The rock and roll lifestyle had taken a heavy toll on him and he now seemed completely incapable of making any commercially sound decision. The company had not signed a new band for over a decade and now survived only on revenue from it's extensive historic back-catalogue.

"The Russians have restarted his basic metabolism, but as we know they can't repair his higher brain functions," she explained.

"Sure," Kane smiled, "I just want to know when I can talk to Lenny LeMort."

"You'll never be able to talk to him," Stella replied, trying to hide her exasperation. "Lenny died over thirty years ago from an overdose. Because he was buried in an airtight sarcophagus his body was well preserved, and the Russians have been able to restart his basic motor functions using modern technology so it can breathe, digest and so blood flows. But the brain can't be restarted, so Lenny will still be literally brain dead."

"He was brain dead through most of his career but we still got four platinum albums and ten number one hits out of him," countered Kane.

"He won't be able to sing, talk or even think. The best we can hope for is that he can stand, and possibly walk a few steps."

"So all we need to do is arrange the dates and venues for his comeback tour," Kane enthused. "Lenny LeMort Live!"

"It'll be a lot more complicated than that," Stella reminded him, knowing she would have to do the vast majority of what seemed to be an impossible task.

"Yeah, yeah," said Kane, his attention already returning to the X-Box. "You'd best make a start: let's not keep the fans waiting too long!"

Even Stella had underestimated the scale of what was needed. Resurrecting a long-dead rock legend was the stuff of science fiction, and neither international law nor domestic regulations were remotely capable of being able to deal with the reality of what Ed Kane envisaged. Society and the media were even more of a challenge; the unpredictability of both being a dangerous unknown. Lenny LeMort would be considered to be either an amazing marvel of science, or else a sick and degrading commercial exercise to make money from a re-animated corpse. After weeks of deliberation between Kane's small team of legal advisors, accountants and spin-doctors they were still nowhere near a clear consensus about what to do next. In frustration Stella decided to take the initiative, as usual. She knew Kane was usually at his most receptive after his forth tequila of the day, so waited until noon to go and see him. She took her usual deep breath before knocking loudly at his office door and walking in.

"Just the person!" Kane announced, without taking his eyes from the huge TV screen which dominated the far wall. "I need your advice."

"Okay," replied Stella unenthusiastically.

"Should I use a shotgun or grenades to clear the zombies from the cell block ahead?"

Stella sighed, glancing at the grim prison yard displayed on the massive gaming display. Once he moved his character into the barricaded building she knew he would give her no time whatsoever. "Before you go in, I'd like to talk to you about Lenny LeMort," she said.

"Yeah, absolutely!" cried Kane, turning to face her. "Have you booked the date for the concert yet?"

"There are some insurmountable problems regarding the resurrection of long-dead rock stars. This means that we can't host the first gig in the UK, the States, or most of Europe, due to their legal frameworks. The best option is to actually stage the initial gig in Russia. Lenny is already there so we won't have any passport issues, and it's a place where legal obstacles can always be crossed by greasing the right palms."

"But I hate Russia!" cried Kane indignantly.

"That may be so," explained Stella, "but it's the only place where we can pull off an early gig. Lenny still has a large core of fans there, and it will be much easier to spin the promotion and manage how we announce his comeback. We publicise the concert in Russia, and if it's a success we look at rolling out in Europe and the US."

"What do you mean 'if'?" Kane challenged. "Lenny made every concert a success!"

"He did when he was alive," countered Stella darkly. "The Russians believe he's now ready and have invited us over next week to see him. I think we'll know then what the chances of success are."

"Cool," smiled Kane, "I can't wait to see him."

"I'll get it organised," murmured Stella.

"Before you go, what about clearing the zombies?" asked Kane, motioning with the game controller to the huge screen.

"RPGs," Stella replied flatly.

"Rock and roll!" shouted Kane, punching the air enthusiastically.

The ride from the airport to the laboratories was enough to dampen even Kane's juvenile high spirits. Kraznagorsk would have been an ugly and depressing city on the most pleasantly sunny day of the year, but in the freezing February fog it took on a mind-numbingly dismal aspect. No one spoke until the large black Mercedes pulled off the potholed road and parked in a deserted parking lot by an anomalous concrete building.

"This doesn't look good," muttered Charlie Hix, peering over his horn-rimmed spectacles. Hix was Kane's accountant, and always attended if there was any danger of Kane squandering any more of the company's increasingly scarce cash.

"Have a swig of this, Charlie," said Kane as he held his hip flask out. "Guaranteed to warn your cockles!"

Hix politely declined. Although he had been Kane's personal accountant for over twenty years, Kane never seemed to realise that Hix never drank alcohol.

"What about you Stella?" Kane asked.

Even though Stella did drink alcohol, she knew better than to sample anything from Kane's flask. "I'm fine, thanks," she said with a forced smile.

"Well, I bet Lenny will have a drink with me! 'Ere, Boris, is Lenny inside?" Kane shouted, tapping the silver hip flask against the dark smoked glass which separated them from the driver.

The driver ignored the tapping, looking instead

out of his right window towards the building. As if on cue, two figures exited through a small doorway and headed towards them. Both were huddled in heavy jackets against the cold winter chill. The driver quickly got out and opened the door next to Kane, the resultant wave of cold air making the occupants instantly shiver. Kane hesitantly exited the cavernous Mercedes to meet the approaching Russians, slowly followed by Stella and Hix.

"Mister Kane," said the first figure in a heavy accent from behind the upturned collar of his heavy woollen jacket. "It's good to meet you at last. I'm the head of the Kraznaorsk Research: Doctor Boris Arsenyev."

"Boris!" laughed Kane. "Aren't you all called Boris in Russia?"

"No," replied Arsenyev, a look of slight puzzlement on his broad face. "This is Doctor Pietor Romanienko, Lenny LeMort's personal physician."

"Cool," said Kane, instantly forgetting both their names. "This is my Personal Assistant, Stella, and this is Charlie Hix, my bean counter."

"Accountant," corrected Hix, shaking the gloved hands of the two Russians.

"Please follow me," said Arsenyev, leading them quickly towards the small door in the concrete building.

They entered a sparse reception, manned by a stern faced man who looked he doubled as security. By the door stood two security guards who looked like they doubled as stern faced men. Arsenyev led them down a wide corridor, the shiny white tiles on the floor and walls reflecting the glare from the un-shaded lights overhead. Sterile and devoid of any decoration, the place looked like an austere and under funded hospital. A peculiar smell also pervaded the building; an odour that noone could quite place.

"My office is just down here," explained Arsenyev from the front. "Let's take some coffee and discuss the next steps."

"Wait!" cried Kane, stopping dead in his tracks. "I didn't come half way around the world for coffee. I had enough of that on the plane. I want to see Lenny before we do anything else!"

Arsenyev glanced quizzically at Romanienko, who replied with a silent nod.

"As you wish," Arsenyev conceded. "As we have made clear in our previous correspondence, due to the length of time Lenny was dead and the condition within the sarcophagus, we have had to commit a lot more time and resources."

"We have already made the final payment," blurted out Hix, Kane's Accountant. "We are not paying a rubel more!"

"Of course not," nodded Arsenyev gravely. "I merely wanted to point out that although he died from a drug overdose, his physical condition before death was not good. We found advanced scirrocis of the liver, lung disease and ghonnarea to start with. Most of his smaller blood vessels were also damaged beyond repair. He has been given a liver transplant, a pacemaker, and his gall bladder has been removed, but the physical condition of his skin, tissue and many of his internal organs is poor. Despite our best efforts we don't think his body will remain physically stable for more than six months."

"So, we've got six months to try and recuperate our investment," Hix said pointedly to Kane.

"That's not long," sighed Stella.

"If we can't recuperate our investment, when Lenny goes down so will EK records," muttered Hix.

"But there is some good news," Arsenyev cut in. "Incredibly, he retains some higher brain functions. He has the capability of basic speech and rudimentary thought!"

"What?" gasped Stella. "You said that was impossible!"

"Normally it is," Arsenyev replied. "But we think the chemicals in the drugs he habitually took built up in his brain. These chemicals, known as TTVFTs, formed a semi-protective layer in some areas, preserving the neurones and synapses which normally perish."

"Thank God for drugs!" Kane enthused, seemingly oblivious to the irony that it was the drugs that killed him in the first place.

"He's in this room to the right," said Romanienko, moving forwards and punching in a code into a keypad by a closed door.

The lock clicked open and Romanienko walked inside, holding the door open for the others to enter. Two stout orderlies in white overalls sat playing chess at a table in the middle of the white tiled room. They stood up as Arsenyev entered and moved silently to the side. The third occupant sat motionless in a large chair by the far wall. Dressed only in a large poncho-like medical gown, Lenny LeMort stared blankly ahead with glazed and watery eyes.

"Lenny!" cried Kane, running over to the long dead singer.

The two orderlies moved to intercept, stopping him before he reached Lenny. With obvious indignation Kane looked over their shoulders to take in the financial future of his company. Stella also stared at Lenny, in fact she could not take her eyes off him. She instantly recognised the star from the myriad of posters and pictures at EK Records, and the often played videos, but there was something terribly wrong.

His skin was mottled and waxy, a network of dark veins below the surface giving it the appearance of blue cheese. His arms and legs were matchstick thin, the muscles seemingly wasted and desiccated beneath their taut pallid cover. Her eyes were then drawn to what she first thought were painted fingernails, but slowly realised she was looking at the tips of protruding yellowed bones poking through the decayed skin of each digit. She gagged and took a step backwards, then gagged again as she realised the dead eyes were following her.

"He looks great!" cried Kane, trying in vain to push past the two orderlies.

Stella exchanged a horrified glance with Hix, who seemed to have turned a pale shade of green.

"This is insane; he looks horrific," Hix stuttered, holding his hand over his mouth.

"I've seen him much worse than this; with makeup and the right clothes he'll look better than he did thirty-five years ago!" Kane gushed. "Let me get closer!"

The two orderlies backed a few feet, but still stood between Kane and his protégée. As Kane neared Lenny ponderously tried to stand. The room went silent as all watched the resurrected star slowly and stiffly rise. Lenny appeared to focus through thick cataracts on his old manager, and started to laboriously move his mouth. All leaned forward to listen, but no noise came. Undeterred, he tried gain, staring straight into Kane's eyes.

"Mama!"

Kane stared in astonishment at Lenny, open mouth and stunned. "This has got to be the happiest day of my life," he blubbered, a tear starting to slowly trickle down his cheek.

On the day they first saw Lenny they had finally agreed to stage the first concert just a month later, to be held locally in Kraznagorsk. Stella had been mortified with the short deadline, but arranging the inaugural event actually proved much easier than she had feared. Rules seemed much easier to bend in Russia, and as long as payment was made in advance it did not seem to matter what she wanted to do with the venue. The other surprise was the speed in which the tickets sold out. Stella knew Lenny had a huge following in the former Soviet states, but had not expected all four thousand to be snapped up within an hour of going on sale with hardly any advertising. Only one small press release had been made, deliberately opaque and lacking in detail, and social media and word-of-mouth had done the rest.

In the hours before the gates opened, Stella grew more and more nervous. Her only concerns revolved around Lenny. Everything else was fine; the backing musicians and singers hired were incredible, the venue great, and all the arrangements perfectly in place. Lenny was driven the short drive to the Kraznagorsk Arena by Doctor Romanienko's small team, who had continued to care and prepare him since the first visit. No further progress had been made as regards speech and motor functions, but the fact Lenny had a vocabulary of about six words was seen as a major achievement by the doctor. Romanienko's main concerns revolved around what Lenny's reaction would be to the noise, lights and huge crowd in the arena, and how long he could remain on his feet.

With less than ten minutes before the concert was due to start, Stella returned once again to the room where Lenny was held. The star of the show sat in a large chair in the middle of the room. On his left, one of Romanienko's orderlies was patiently spoon-feeding a disgusting looking mush into Lenny's compliant mouth, whilst to the right the make-up artist was airbrushing one of his eyebrows back in place.

Stella no longer felt repulsed by Lenny; instead she felt a deep sadness. She had also lost the bitterness she felt towards Ed Kane for going ahead with the charade; now she realised that the old fool genuinely wanted nothing more than to be reunited with his old protégé and to try and recapture some of the magic of days long gone. But the only magic in the sterile room was the spectre created by a science limited only by the money and completely lacking any scruples.

"He looks like a million dollars!" Kane enthused.

"More like fifty million," muttered Hix, glancing up from his laptop.

Stella nodded sadly. The make-up and clothes did capture some of Lenny's former glory, but close up it was hard to mask the signs of decay. Beneath the makeup the skin was gray and dead; the weakened body continually losing ground to the ravaging advances of decay despite the huge doses of antibiotics and white blood cells which Romanienko constantly pumped in. But what she really worried about was what was going on in the remains of Lenny's mind. His vocabulary had remained at only half a dozen words, and he still said 'mama' each time he saw Kane. Kane constantly said that Lenny always looked happy, although Romanienko had explained the permanent half-smile on Lenny's face was really the result of facial muscle atrophy. He had the mental capacity of a small baby, but when shown a stage or played one of his old songs he seemed to change. Instead of his normal look of slight bewilderment he would focus on the stage, and even nod his head in time with the music. Every time she saw it she had to fight back a tear of sadness.

Lenny's apparent recognition of his music pleased Kane and Hix no end, both convinced that it would add significantly to the show. Although the instruments would be live, the vocals were actually recordings from three decades previous. The best they hoped for was that Lenny would manage to stand centre-stage for four or five tracks, and that the audience would see it was really him. Anything else would be a bonus, and would hasten the returns on their heavy investment.

A sudden booming heralded the musicians had finally taken to the stage.

"I'm on!" yelped Kane. "Remember, after my introduction I'll give the signal and you two lead Lenny onto the stage."

Hix and Stella nodded. As Kane bolted through the door they moved towards the seated star. Lenny seemed to know something was happening and slowly started to rise.

"That's the spirit!" said Hix. "The noise is all for you."

Stella took Lenny's right arm and Hix took his left. Although only a short distance it was a slow walk. Lenny shuffled forward, each small step a physical and mental effort to work the shrivelled muscles. The noise from the stage grew louder; a cacophony of cheers and shouts from the capacity crowd. Lenny seemed to hear it, and his pace quickened slightly. Eventually they turned into the stage wings and the noise became deafening. At the front of the stage they could see Kane, milking the crowd and revelling in the applause.

"Good evening Russia!" Kane's voice boomed from the multiple speakers. "Tonight we will witness history. Tonight will be something you will never forget, something you will never tire of telling your children and children's children for as long as you live. For thirty years the World has mourned the tragic loss of Lenny LeMort, cruelly taken in his finest hour. He left a rock and roll legacy that has never been bettered, and created a legend that modern rock stars can only dream about. But tonight, for the first time, I can reveal a true miracle of Russian science!"

Kane paused as the crowd roared, savouring every moment as he waited to speak again.

"Six months ago we brought the sealed sarcophagus of Lenny LeMort here to Kraznagorsk. We had a dream, a vision unlike any other in the history of rock, and we enlisted the help of an incredible team of scientists to turn that dream into reality. The team worked tirelessly, unfettered by convention and rules, and have succeeded in making that dream come true. By the miracle of science and free-thinking, blood flows again in the long dead arteries and air fills the lungs which have not breathed for thirty years. In defiance of the established laws of nature, history has been made and a legend resurrected! Ladies and Gentlemen, please welcome Lenny LeMort!"

The band sprang into action; squealing guitars and the thunder of amplified drums competing against the expectant roar of the crowd. Stella felt a sudden shiver pass through Lenny, the shock causing her to let go of his arm. Without guidance he started to move forwards on his own, the previous shuffling gait replaced by a faster but unsteady walk, limping towards the glare of arcing strobe lights and blinding pyrotechnics.

Hix shouted something but words were drowned out by the opening chords of one of Lenny's biggest hits. The crowd went wild as they saw him, chanting Lenny's name and screaming. Kane stepped aside as Lenny moved to the front of the stage, the flashing lights reflecting from his shiny leather and spandex outfit. Kane yelled encouragement but the words were lost in the roaring cacophony of heavy rock and frantic cheering. Lenny ignored him, staring through heavy cataracts at the packed audience, the sight and sounds seeming to somehow energise his fragile physical frame. As the dubbed opening lyrics poured from the multiple speakers he raised his arms in salute, his lips moving in time with the taped words.

"My god!" Hix shouted at Stella. "Look!"

Stella stared at Lenny, shocked at how the concert was animating him. Lenny started to painfully strut around the front of the stage, punching the air in time to the pounding music. She turned to look at Romanienko, who appeared completely dumbstruck by the scene unfolding on the stage.

"Absolutely unbelievable!" yelled Kane, rejoining them off stage. "The crowd love him! There'll be no stopping us now; this show will conquer the world. We're going to make an absolute fortune!"

The first song finished with a huge crescendo, leaving only the cheering filling the auditorium. Lenny looked confused that the music had stopped and swayed a little, suddenly unsteady again.

"It's the music that's invigorating him," Romanienko yelled at Kane. "Start the next song now!"

Kane looked blankly at the doctor, and then he suddenly understood. He rushed forward towards the lead guitarist but as he did so Lenny swayed again and pitched head first off the stage into the writhing audience. The crowd surged excitedly forward, all eager to support their idol in his first stage dive for three decades. Kane screamed as Lenny disappeared from sight in the sea of roaring fans. Stella, Hix and Romanienko ran towards the edge of the stage, the Russian frantically trying to get security to rescue the star from the heaving swell. Five burly guards jumped into the crowd but seemed powerless in the crush. The stage manager stopped the strobes and switched on the full lighting, killing the pyrotechnics and power to the band's instruments at the same time, but still Lenny didn't resurface.

Only when the fire alarms were activated did the crowd move back, and by that time it was far too late. Lenny had literally fallen apart in the heavy ocean of fans, body parts quickly coming adrift in the turmoil and confusion. When the crowd eventually started to disperse it was clear that little actually remained of the rock star, most of his clothes and his body having been claimed by his ardent fans. After twenty minutes of frantic searching all Kane, Hix, and Stella had was a ripped off ear, two fingers, and the tattered blood-stained sleeve of his leather jacket. Everything else had gone; skin, bone, organs, and even the titanium pacemaker.

Stella walked over to Kane, who stood in the middle of the hall looking forlornly down at the two torn fingers he held in his palm.

"It's over Ed," she said as gently as she could. "Perhaps we should go."

"Did you see him?" Kane sobbed. "Out there on the stage it was like it was in his genes to perform."

Stella nodded, wondering what to do with the severed ear she carried.

"Lenny was incredible!" Kane continued, wiping away his tears.

"He was, but I think it's time to move on," Stella soothed.

"Absolutely right!" Kane cried with sudden enthusiasm. "I want you to see if we can get our hands on Kurt Cobain, John Lennon and Elvis. Long live rock and roll!"

.·

After thirty years at sea, *Ross Baxter* now concentrates on writing sci-fi and horror fiction. His varied work has been published in print by a number of publishing houses in US and UK short story anthologies. In December 2014 he won the Horror Novel Review.Com best short fiction prize. Married to a Norwegian and with two Anglo-Viking kids, he now lives in Derby, England.

Reaper's Program

Noah Page

Dr. Cloak fine tunes the settings on his prototype sensory project after his last subject leaves. Though once he had been proud of his achievements in the field of sensory projection, he now loathed the current circumstances he worked in. Years ago Dr. Cloak and his colleagues had used sensory tech to expose humans to any specific situation without fear of possible physical damage. This led to a range of possibilities: newly recruited cops could be trained to face the reality of emergency situations to see if they were capable of handling the pressure, while prospective mothers could experience childbirth in anticipation of the real thing. But when private companies began to buy the patent for private use, shrewd businesspeople came to see the possibilities for entertainment media in sensory tech. Within months the first "experience theatres" were built, and dozens of people in their own sensory projectors would share in perceptual reproductions of the Titanic sinking, the first moon landing, or riding down the steppes of Asia with the Mongol armies. Particularly savvy entrepreneurs came up with the idea of exploiting the most base natures of humanity, and soon sleazy clubs and bars were advertising with lurid signs promising "An hour in paradise only 50 dollars!" or "15 minutes in a two-some or until you cum—20 dollars!"

Dr. Cloak had come to believe that these would be the worst uses of projection tech, but the spread of sensory video games proved him wrong entirely. Kids with wealthy parents and private projectors would spend hours and sometimes days absorbed in castle sieges or fast paced dog fights with futuristic jets. The arcade became an extremely profitable business again, as the price for even the lowest quality projector was astronomically high. Terrible behaviour became a frequent feature of these arcades. Children would cry and scream for hours after their parents forced them away from the games, and teenagers would refuse to leave when the managers tried to kick them out at the end of the day. When more and more incidents like these occurred, mental health professionals became convinced that a sensory program could be written that would make any projector junkie into a responsible and obedient youth, and so Dr. Cloak dedicated himself to research in the fight against sensory addiction.

An assistant nurse enters as Dr. Cloak finishes tinkering with the projector. She hands the doctor a clipboard with the next subject's information and begins to organize the doctor's notes from his last test.

"How did the last subject respond to the program?" the nurse asks.

"Very well. Very well indeed. He said himself

that he now understands how dangerous his habits were and why his parents were so eager to make him quit," Dr. Cloak replies as he begins ticking boxes and writing notes on his next patients forms.

"That's fantastic to hear. It seems kids are becoming worse and worse every day. Yesterday I walked by the arcade on Gibson Street, and there were cop cars and an ambulance parked outside."

"What happened?" Dr. Cloak says as he glances up from his forms.

"A young man apparently bit off the earlobe of his girlfriend when she refused to give him more money to play." Dr. Cloak shudders, then removes his glasses and begins massaging his temples.

"That will be all, Beth. Send in the next subject," he says without looking at her.

"Uh, doctor, there's something you should know about the next subject."

"What is it?"

"He doesn't know why he's really here. He seems to think that he's here to test a new game... something about a bloody mandible?"

"That's enough, Beth. Send him in and I'll deal with him myself," Dr. Cloak says.

Moments later the nurse ushers Haytees in the office. At first the unkempt, smelly teenager is fascinated by the exposed electronics of the prototype projector, but then becomes confused when he notices that the wrinkled and bald Dr. Cloak is apparently the leading the play tests for Blood Crucible 4. The young man and the old doctor stare each other down for a few moments.

"You must be Haytees Underson," Dr. Cloak finally says. "I'm Dr. Cloak, and I'll be running you through this stimulation simulation today, but before we start we're going to have a talk and I'll ask you a few questions."

"Whatever, make it quick. I'm bored already, and I only came here to test Blood Crucible 4, not to talk with anyone. Writing your stupid application cut into enough of my arcade time already."

Dr. Cloak winces, and instantly fears that this will reveal his disgust for sensory games to his subject. Haytees doesn't pay much attention him, though. Dr. Cloak then tries to hide his shock at Haytees's disrespect towards him. Most of his subjects so far had been teary-eyed girls and boys who would hang their heads in shame when they talked about their problems.

Then it strikes the doctor why this teen was demanding to test a videogame-his parents had fooled him into being a subject by promising the boy that he would be testing a new game!

It's an awfully cunning trick on their part, Dr. Cloak thinks to himself, but I certainly wish his parents had told me beforehand. Dr. Cloak realizes that Haytees could be a solution to the problem he had been having with the program. His regular subjects would usually form an incomplete basis for the program, but a person who believed he was playing a videogame might be willing to give a much clearer picture. Dr. Cloak does his best to shake himself out of his quiet elation, and starts to ask the usual pre-program questions in a hurry.

"Alright, I'll try to make this quick then. On

average how much time a day do you spend playing games in sensory projectors?"

"About eight or nine hours."

"And where do you get the money to play?"

"I have a part time job for a few hours a day. Luckily it's right next to the arcade with the best games, so I don't have to spend time getting there."

"So you spend eight hours a day in the arcade and another few at work? Do you still go to school? Do you have friends you play sports with perhaps?"

"My only friends are other players. I suppose I haven't been to school in a long time," Haytees mumbles and shuts his eyes. "I don't need to go anyway. I'm going to go pro in Destruction Force once I can find some teammates who don't suck." Haytees's eyes spring open and he glares at Dr. Cloak. "I don't really have time for these questions. If you're not going to let me play, I'm not going to waste my time hanging around here talking to you. Why do you even care if I go to school or not?"

Dr. Cloak sighs, then forces a bitter smile in reaction to Haytees's belligerent impatience. He leads his subject towards the sensory projector-an upright cushioned pod with restraints for the arms and legs inside of it. A long pole with ten slightly shimmering knobs protruding from it sits upright next to the pod.

Dr. Cloak motions Haytees to enter the pod, but Haytees instead stops, and stares at the odd, faintly glowing knobs.

"I've never seen the mechanical bits of a projector before. Kids usually break 'em during their temper tantrums, so the arcades usually make sure that all the flimsy parts like these are, I don't know, hidden in the walls or something. Can you show me how it works?"

Dr. Cloak twists his face into a distrusting frown. Why does he care how the sensory projector works? Dr. Cloak wonders to himself. He probably wants to tamper with the projectors in the arcades, for a meagre increase in score or some other childish goal.

"I'll give you the layman explanation, though I doubt you'll even understand that," Dr. Cloak says before pointing to the lower row of five knobs. "These five knobs are the actual sensory projectors. They essentially transmit a mimic neural signal to the brain, one which makes the mind believe it is experiencing the sensory perception in question." Dr. Cloak pauses, pulls out a cloth from his pocket, takes off his glasses and polishes them before continuing. "These knobs here are what makes this projector unique, and what make, uh, Red Crucible 3 such an amazing breakthrough in sensory gaming. They allow this device to pull sensory data from the memory of the player, and recreate the exact situation the player was remembering."

Haytees eyes Dr. Cloak with suspicion, and he almost asks why the doctor can't even remember the name of the game he's supposed to be testing, but his excitement about being the one of the first people to try such a radically innovative concept stops him. "So what are you going to use that for, to simulate my ideal battlefield to kill demons on?" Haytees asks instead.

Dr. Cloak laughs at the absurdity of using his

new technology for such a shallow pursuit, but abruptly stops when he realizes that he had laughed in the same way when he first heard that sensory projectors were going to be used for sensory gaming. "No, nothing like that," Dr. Cloak says as he crosses to his computer in the corner of the room and sits down in front of it. "Why don't you get in the restraints and I'll explain the rest before the isolation pod is closed."

Haytees stands in front of the open pod, looking down at the restraints that he knew had stopped his limbs from jerking around during particularly intense matches. His stomach grows tight with an unexplainable dread as braces himself against the back of the pod and places his arms and legs in the padded steel cuffs. Before Haytees can consider the source of this unexpected apprehension, the cuffs snap shut on him.

"When the isolation pod closes on you, I want to think of the moment you were happiest in life. I want you to imagine every feeling on your skin, every scent in the air, the taste of air food that you might have been eating, every sound that you heard. I want you to see every colour, texture, and shape you can remember. The more detailed the memory, the more complete the recreation will be."

"What the hell does this have to do with Blood Crucible 4?" Haytees asks as his stomach grows even more shriveled with tension.

"Well... you're going to defend the thing you love most," Dr. Cloak improvises. "It makes you fight harder than ever, and the more vivid the memory is the more vicious and violentyou'll act to protect it. I'm going to shut the chamber now, and I'll give you a few minutes to think of moment you were happiest, then it will take a few more minutes for the sensor to do its scan, and after that I'll begin the simulation."

The pod door swings closed on Haytees, just as he realizes Dr. Cloak must have been lying about something, but his wonder about the simulation is greater than his fear of deception, so he begins to daydream about a brighter past.

Many poets and philosophers have tried to describe the curious entrance to a sensory projector simulation. The most apt analogy is that it is like going to sleep and suddenly finding yourself dreaming of some absurd situation or location but being completely convinced that it's real. This is Haytees exact reaction when he finds himself in an unbelievably accurate recreation of the small, seaside beach where he spent most of his last summer before he had moved away to the city where he lived now. Because the simulation was drawn directly from Haytees's memory, he had no reason not to believe that this wasn't the very moment he had been remembering only mere moments ago.

The sand beneath his feat is hot and coarse, and his damp bathing suit clings to his legs, causing droplets of water to slide down to his ankles. A mild breeze sends the scent of saltwater past his face, and makes gentle waves lap at the shore. Above him, sparse clouds drift past the blazing sun while seagulls squawk and swoop over the vast waters. For the first time in months, Haytees doesn't feel angry at anything, and doesn't feel the need to be winning at something.

He takes a deep breath, and exhales a blissful sigh.

In the recreation of the memory, Haytees's now ex-girlfriend Stephanie came towards him with a bottle of sun screen in her hands. Though in the present Haytees and Stephanie hadn't seen each other for years, the simulation persuaded him that they were still together. He thinks that they still love each other, and he has no reason not to.

"Hey, I found a little more in this bottle. Can you get my back?" Stephanie smiles mischievously, then continues, "maybe if you're really good I'll let you do my thighs."

Haytees feels his penis harden, just as he did when all this actually happened. Stephanie's hair is messy from swimming, and her pale, freckled face was beginning to redden from the sun.

She gives Haytees the bottle and turns. He squeezes the last handful into his hands, then rubs it on her shoulders, down the curve of her back, and finally on her hips. She turns back towards him, cups his cheeks with her hands, and leans in to kiss him. Her lips are stained with a faded purple from the blueberries she had been eating earlier, and her mouth tastes like them to.

It's perfect-a simply indiscernible lie.

"So you're leaving tomorrow, huh?" she says as she wraps her arms around his waist.

"Yeah."

"We can't be together anymore, you know that, right? You're practically on the other side of the country. I have enough trouble when I can't see you every day."

"Yeah. I know. I don't want to go. I want to stay here with you. There's nothing I can do without you. Nobody understands me except you." He feels tears begin to prickle in his eyes, butStephanie wipes them away before he can really start to cry.

"C'mon, don't worry about it. You're smarter and cooler and more fun than you think you are. I know you'll make new friends really fast."

"Yeah. I'll be fine. If you think I'm going to be okay, then I know I'm going to be okay."

"Anyway, let's not think about that right now. We got the rest of today, and," she pauses and smiles her coy smile again, "we've got tonight."

In the real memory, Stephanie would go to sunbathe on the big pink towel she had lain down hours before. But the aura of a dark cloak sweeps across the simulation, and instead she begins to walk slowly towards where the beach meets the sea. There she stops, and gazes over her shoulder at Haytees.

"Goodbye, Haytees," she whispers as she dips her feet into the water. She immerses herself up to her knees in the warm water, then launches her whole body in, and starts to swim towards the horizon.

Haytees wants to follow her, but finds his body is immobilized. He wants to call after Stephanie, begging her to come back, but finds he has lost his voice as well.

"This isn't how it happened," is all he manages to murmur.

Stephanie swims further and further away from him, until he can no longer see her – only the long, curving line of the horizon. He expects to be miserable, or bitter, or angry and competitive, but instead there is nothing.

The nothing starts to consume him.

It's strange, because Haytees is aware that something is absent, but he can't place what the absence is. Then he realizes that he can no longer feel the rough heat of the sand between his toes. As he is wondering where the feeling in his skin had gone, the sound of the waves slapping against the shore vanishes as well, and there is no more salty breeze filling his nose. After that, it was like the great light switch of the world had been flipped off, and Haytees's sight of the gulls and clouds and sun are replaced by blindness. Finally, the vague taste of blueberries is gone, and with that, Haytees outward perception is no more.

Because Haytees's mind is convinced that the outside world no longer existed, it convinces itself that it did not exist either, and this is like death. This is a soundless drop past fading layers of memory, perception and consciousness, into a void where the self is a no longer a thing, where the very idea of there being a self at all is impossible to create.

The pod door swings open, and the restraints around Haytees's arms and legs unlock. He stands there without stepping out of the pod, trembling slightly and shaking his head. His forehead is slick with perspiration, as though he had just woken from a terrible fever dream.

"How do you feel, Haytees?" Dr. Cloak asks.

"I don't know. I don't understand. I think I've lost every important game I've ever played. I've lost every game that mattered."

"Oh. I see. Well, I wasn't completely honest with you, Haytees. You see I'm trying to write a program that will break an adolescent's addiction to sensory projection games. The program was meant to give you the best part of your life, then suddenly take it away, and make you believe you had died. In this way I hoped to demonstrate the shortness and preciousness of life.

"Ninety percent of young people who experienced this program had a renewed sense of ambition and motivation, and often felt no desire to waste time playing sensory games. Do you feel a new inspiration to go back to school now, and find a career that will benefit yourself and society?"

Haytees and Dr. Cloak lock eyes. The young man's gaze is flat, and without any trace of emotion.

"No, no, not at all. I feel like any win I get doesn't even matter because the only game I really know, the only game we all know, always ends in a loss."

Dr. Cloak flinches in horror. Never before in two hundred and thirty-seven tests had a subject been so adversely affected by the program. Terrible thoughts filled his mind—would this be the end of any notion that the program could be mass distributed? Would his license be revoked for causing such trauma to someone? And what about the boy: if Haytees could not recover, would the boy's parents sue him?

"Why don't you... why don't you go talk to your parents about what happened. I'm sure you'll feel better after a nutritious dinner and a good night's sleep." Dr. Cloak stutters as he reaches for his phone and begins to dial his lawyer's number.

But Haytees can find no solace in such a simple suggestion. All he can feel was the grey cloud of death hovering right above his head, always threatening to burst into a rain storm and wash him away into nothingness.

∴

Noah Page is a recent graduate from the University of New Brunswick Fredericton, holding a degree in Honours English. He has published with Viator, Calliope, UNB's Journal of Student Writing, and had poetry featured in The City Series: Fredericton chapbook published by Frog Hollow editions. He was the recipient of UNB's Charles G.D. Roberts prize in 2015 for his short story "The party doesn't stop for you".

Your Actual Vermin

Stephen McQuiggan

"Taylor's off work," said Rory.

Frank spat out a large chunk of apple, feeling it turn to ashes in his mouth; off work—how he hated that euphemism. He could picture Taylor now, sweating and salivating in a lab, wired up like a plug, waiting on that long cold needle they...

He wound down the window and threw out the half eaten core, his hunger forcibly evicted. "Yeah, well," he sighed, "he must have let his guard down."

"You have to keep your wits about you," agreed Rory. That was rule number one of the GermXterm handbook: Never drop your guard.

The van coughed and spluttered as Rory cranked his way through the gears, each one as crotchety and stubborn as he, and the traps and the poisons rattled in the back in protest.

If that sour bastard ever cracked a smile, thought Frank, I think the world would end. Listening to his colleague grumbling under his breath as they waited for the lights to change, Frank wondered for the umpteenth time why he had to be saddled with a guy whose face could turn milk.

There were times when he yearned to sign up for the Rats and Bats brigade, but he knew better than to request a transfer. The lads of the Prosaic Pest Division were underpaid, and held in sneering contempt by the Ultra Vermin crew; cowards, part timers—Bugs N Slugs Rory called them.

Those pangs returned when he had been issued with today's assignment. He thought he would happily take any abuse his workmates heaped upon him if only he didn't have to make a trip to the Chamberfell estate. He could vividly recall his first day on the job, eager and green as Irish snot; how noble he had felt, a 'servant of the community', a 'protector of the innocent', just like it said on his coveralls. That kind of naïve bullshit was as dangerous as the factory where they were heading.

For all his faults, Rory had taken him under his wing from the get go, and the old basset hound's street smarts had saved his life on more than one occasion. There was a camaraderie amongst the Ultra Vermin crew that could never be replicated in any other line of work and, despite his misgivings, he knew he could never abandon his calling.

Frank watched the streets glide by, a hazy stream of luminous greens and ill purples, polluted channels of flickering neon peopled by stick figures rummaging through endless mounds of rubbish, soiling the air by their very presence.

They were close to the Fifth Sector, or the Filth Sector as it was known back at base. The police helicopters hovered relentlessly above, their searchlights dancing across the rooftops. This part of the city was a haven for vermin; hybrids and mutants that shared little in common save their capacity to spread disease. Frank felt the first real stirrings of unease penetrate his habitual vague numbness.

"It's hard to credit there was a time when a callout meant salting a few slugs, bashing a few rodents," said Rory, as if relating fresh insight on the trade instead of rehashing a favourite yarn. "Course, when I say rodents I'm not talking about the ones we have now. I'm talking tiddlers. Why, the biggest would be craning its neck to stare a rabbit in the eye."

The mention of rabbits caused Frank to avert his gaze from his grizzled partner. He hated the constant reminders of things that were gone that could never be again—rabbits, birds, fish. He couldn't recall the last time he had seen a dog.

"Yeah, those were the days alright," mused Rory. "Before the buggers mutated into the flesh eating ponies we have now. All you needed was a trap, a hunk of cheese, and Bob's your auntie's live in lover." Rory paused, lost in the simplicity of a bygone age. "Now rats are a minor irritation compared to what we've got to—"

"Please put on your Auto Purge helmets and reset your toxin indicators," chimed the metallic voice from the digi-dash, nipping Rory's nostalgia in the bud. "Site of infestation one click north east."

A small red dot pulsed satanically on the scanner, marking the location of the factory that had sent out the distress call. Rory swung the van into the vast parking lot of Holden's Oats, coming to a halt in front of its austere entrance; the factory loomed over them, hunched with intent.

"No puppy rats for us," sighed Rory, nestling his round head snugly into his helmet and drawing his Flash gun to check it was charged. "What we're dealing with here is your actual vermin."

There was a soft hiss as the van doors lifted, casting an insectile silhouette on the tarmac beneath the flickering lamplights. On the radio mic inside his helmet Frank could hear Rory muttering to himself as he clambered out from behind the steering rod; in his oversize white uniform he resembled a wizened pea in a space age pod. Double checking their wrist dials for sign of nearby activity, they gave each other the thumbs up before heading down the stairwell into the despatch area signed Sunshine Porridge.

The steps were narrow and slippy, their treachery accentuated by the soupy darkness. Employees 1691XIV and 14CIV of the Ultra Vermin Corps switched on their night-scanners to break up the oppressive pseudo midnight. On their visor monitors they could make out the ethereal frames of the loading bay doors some twenty feet below, swinging silently in a non wind, thick rivulets of slime oozing through their warped hinges, reflecting Day-Glo red on Frank's screen.

There was no one here to meet them.

"We're too late," said Frank.

There was a crackle that always sounded like inappropriate laughter before Rory's voice filled the lonely void in his helmet. "Don't panic, son."

Don't panic.

Another pearl of GermXterm wisdom. They drilled it into during three years basic training: Don't let your guard down; Don't panic; No mercy; No sympathy; Kill on sight. It took a certain type of man to do this job. Not for the first time, Frank got to wondering if he was that type after all.

Rory nudged one of the doors open with the stem of his Flash gun. It swung inward, revealing a large warehouse lit only by the impudent lightning of a row of blinking fluorescents. A smell of dank rot seeped through their mouth grills, lending the space a subterranean feel. The sacks of corn and oatmeal, stacked and awaiting delivery, were busted and torn, spilling their dusty dry guts onto the grey cement floor.

"Bloody bleeding ground," barked Rory. "No wonder they had an outbreak. Place is an accident waiting to happen. I thought the State outlawed shitholes like this, I mean, what the fuck do those Sanitary agents actually do?"

Frank covered his partner's back as the old veteran made his way to the manager's office. When Rory disappeared inside the portakabin he followed, training his weapon on every shadow, every sound. When he entered the small wooden hut the smell made him gag.

"Bastards beat us to him," said Rory, as if stating the time. Frank flicked on the office lights and turned off his monitor, as if the horror on the screen could be rendered meaningless by the reality of his eyes.

The office had been trashed, the work of a savage mind. The plant manager lay amid the debris seemingly in peaceful repose upon a heap of worksheets, still clutching the emergency call button in one rigid hand. His eyes, wide open and staring straight to hell, were glowing yellow.

"He's infected. You know what to do."

"Shouldn't we bring him back to the Lab for testing?" Frank knew he was clutching at straws.

"Christ, son, you know what they'll do to him. Kill him now before he comes round, let him rest in peace, not pieces."

Frank nodded as Rory shuffled by, picking up a clipboard that had a large chunk bitten out of it; "Scum will eat anything," he muttered on his way out the door.

Frank set the Flash to max 8, pointed and fired once, sending the manager's benignly smiling head shooting to the ceiling like a cheap firework; singed meat splashed across his white coverall but slid off without a stain. There had to be an easier way to make a living, he thought, fleeing the hut. He found his partner atop a large mound of oatmeal. He kept his head down in case the old man spotted his tears but Rory's attention was elsewhere.

"Never seen anything like this before." Rory's breath made strange sucking whistles as he spoke. "Never in all my born days."

Frank leaned in closer to see what had so perplexed him; a large number of prints ran over the meal, veering off in all directions.

"Looks like we have a whole family here."

"That it does," agreed Frank flatly.

"We'd best split up. Maintain radio contact every

two minutes and keep your strobe tracker on." Rory's tone alarmed Frank, but the old man vanished down the other side of the mound before he had a chance to question his anxiety.

Keep moving, keep your wits about you.

As Frank set off the stench of decay seemed to pervade his very pores; his skin was oily with sweat, a slick film of corruption. He made his way under a low arch, entering a large mausoleum that housed innumerable machines, prehistoric skeletal giants. They also looked as if they had to be manually operated—the proprietors of Holden's Sunshine Oats had a lot of questions to answer when the reports were filed on this one.

"All clear?" Rory's voice made him jump, seeming to emanate between his own ears.

He drew a ragged breath and lied, "Fine and dandy mate."

Frank wandered on through the maze of mechanical hulks, stumbling across the body of worker after worker, their eyes alerting him to their presence, twin pinpricks of undiluted evil glowing in the gloom. He blasted them all, feeling colder, more clinical than the machinery that bore witness to his carnage.

A shadow scurried to his left. Frank froze; could be just a rat, please god, just a rat, or maybe—.

A childish giggle tinkled in the darkness.

"Rory," he whispered into his mic. "Oh Christ, Rory, I think we've got a real problem here."

"Sit tight son, I'm tracking you right now."

"Hurry, I think—"

And then it was upon him.

It lashed at the dials on his suit with razor claws, spitting venom that splashed and sizzled across his visor, all the while giggling through its pointed little teeth. Frank smashed the stem of his flash gun down hard into the child's face, sending the boy sprawling across the floor, clattering into a wedge of empty plastic silos.

It could only have been seven or eight years old. Its hair, once blonde, now matted black with clotted blood. The boy was naked, grimed in human sludge, and burning with rage. Clenching its tiny fists, it spat a torrent of acid that fell short, smoking gleefully in a pool on the concrete floor. Its eyes burned like nuclear suns.

Frank struck the child again, feeling something in its skull give. It raised one hand up to him in supplication, molten tears careening down its once innocent face.

"Dada?"

For a moment Frank forgot the rules; it was just a kid for Christsake, no different from his little Ben. He reached out a gloved hand to comfort the child and caught a glint of silver as the foot long tusk emerged from the boy's sunken chest; it smiled as the tusk coiled, ready to sting.

Frank aimed and fired, blasting the tiny poisoned frame into the netherworld, painting the surrounding walls green with its vile blood.

No sympathy. No mercy. Kill on sight.

That wasn't a child, that was your actual vermin. It wasn't dead, it had been made redundant. The training mantra ran over and over in his head as he carried on firing; textbook answers to unwritten feelings.

"Nice one." Rory was behind him. "Follow me, I think I've found the Hive."

Frank barely heard him, the waves of breath crashing deafeningly over his teeth.

"Snap out of it!" Rory shoved him hard before moving off, shooting intermittently at random sacks as he did so. Frank followed as if in a dream, catching up with his partner as they reached a set of stairs that spiralled down to a basement as cold and dark as any poetic grave.

"Switch to flame," advised Rory, "and cover my wrinkly ass." He descended into the pit as Frank licked the walls above his head with incandescent fire.

The basement was a portrait of hell, alive with death.

The children—vermin! vermin! Vermin!—were legion here, scurrying over the floor, crawling on the ceiling and the walls, their strange keening an echo somewhere between terror and hate.

Standing back to back they cleansed the area with a routine strafe, watching the meagre bodies fall and crackle, crunching the charred husks as they pursued the smouldering survivors.

"That should do it," panted Rory as the smoke cleared. "Holden Oats well and truly purged. We'll get a bonus and a half for this. There must have been hundreds of the little bug—"

"What about Mother?" asked Frank quietly, unable to equate the calm voice that spoke with the one yammering feverishly in his mind.

There was a large hole in the back wall,

symmetrical like a honeycomb. Rory looked over at it, then nodded to Frank. Though he had never actually seen one before, Frank knew from endless training seminars that this must be the Nursery. He plodded through the portal, an automaton on auto pilot. The vision before him melted away his armour of indifference.

She was beautiful.

Her hair a blazing sunrise, her body the stuff of teenage sweats. She was bent double in the rubble strewn hole, her breathing laboured, her perfect face flushed with exertion as she pushed out egg after skull sized egg onto the dirty floor. She ignored the interlopers, carrying on with the task at hand, knee deep in her gleaming spawn.

Frank lurched as Rory took aim; it was all so wrong, surely something so exquisite had to retain some of its humanity.

"No!" Frank tore off his helmet and threw it at his partner, knocking his arm askew, sending a blue bolt of energy crackling through the ceiling.

Rory spun round, the anger on his face giving way to horror. "Frank, watch—"

A shadow blink and she was on him. Locked in her embrace with her putrid breath on his neck, he felt her poison in his soul and then he felt no more.

He awoke in a white room that refused to stay still. Gradually, as his vision steadied and his senses cleared, he began to pick out details in the nothingness; a vase of synthetic flowers, a wall chart, an IV drip by his bed.

He heard distant voices coming ever closer and, turning his head, saw a man in a bed opposite him. He fought down the nausea and saw nurses, pretty nurses all in a row, attending to his stricken roommate. Something about the patient's haggard face seemed familiar; that crooked nose, those heavy jowls.

"Rory?" croaked Frank. "Rory, is that you?"

Rory turned, a smile on his face. One of the nurses tutted, adjusting her position as she lowered the foot long needle into his eye. His glowing, yellow, demon eye.

Rory screamed.

For a moment Frank wondered how one man could scream so much, then realised he was screaming too.

.·

Stephen McQuiggan was the original author of the bible; he vowed never to write again after the publishers removed the dinosaurs and the spectacular alien abduction ending from the final edit. His first novel, A Pig's View Of Heaven, is available now from Grinning Skull Press.

Don't Open Till Doomsday

Chasing the Fat Man to the Edge

Stephen Scott Whitaker

The Dun-in man pulled his wrap around his face and stalked forward in the snowy wastes. Ahead of him, somewhere in the winter gloom, his prey walked ahead, struggling in the weather. The Dun-in man had been tracking him for three days now, three days going north in the winter. No easy task. But the commandant at the colony wanted the man dead. Wanted the man brought back.

"There's a gold piece in it for you."

The Dun-in man just pointed at the pistol on the commandant's desk, the old .45 Army regulation in the worn canvas holster.

"This?" Karl teased.

The Dun-in man had nodded.

"It's yours if you bring this fat man back to us. Our former leader had his way with our food stores and I want him to suffer. I want that fat man to suffer, you hear me?" Karl laughed cruelly and leaned back in his chair.

The Dun-in man only nodded, and had set out that very afternoon.

The toxic wastes changed constantly, the heavy metal chemicals mutated most things they did not kill. Over the last decade the Dun-in man had seen the last of the northern colonies fall. Out west, the living gathered in cities to bring back industry and agriculture. But out here, in the north, the living gathered to survive, hoping the land would pay them back in kind. Winter brought purple snows and orange glows across the sky. But the snow he trudged through was white. A good sign. It had been a long time since he'd seen pure white snow. He was tempted to bend down like a child and taste it, but refrained. The white flakes glistened and caught the light.

The Dun-in man wore two layers of underclothes under his ripped and patched jeans, and under his wool plaid shirt. They were nearly ten years old, but he kept them together with cotton and wool shirts he'd pick off the rag pile. The deer hide pants and tunic he wore over those clothes was what kept the weather from soaking through to his bones. He'd killed the three animals that made up his skins. And for that he was fortunate. The old commandant had made the mistake of allowing the colony to hunt the deer out.

His long grey wrap which was part wool, part ripstop fabric, had been made by his mother for his father so long ago that it seemed like a dream. It was heavy, but kept the rain off, and could be used as shelter in warmer weather, and a cloak of sorts in colder weather. He gathered it about him, and over his face wrapped in scarves, and over his fur hat. Still the weather gave him pause; he was heading deeper north, in the winter, into the wastes.

The wind picked up, and to his right a bare tree fell. For a second his heart rate increased, and half expected to see someone crashing through the storm towards him. But he did not raise his long rifle. There was no one. Nothing but the wind. There were few beasts left in the deep north; hadn't seen any animal tracks in the last six months of scouting. None. But the north country's soil was queer from the toxins. Perhaps after this pure white winter some life would return. Nature had a way. After all, he was still alive, and those who lived in the colony, and god knows how many more down south and out west. Part of him would love to see a big shaggy wolf tear through the scrub pines filled with snow. To shoot a deadly animal. To sink his knife into its belly. To eat hot meat off a fire. He'd had nothing but ration food since he left camp to chase the fat man.

The fat man had a machete, that was for sure, and whether or not he was armed with a shotgun no one in the colony was certain. For the fat man had been acting "squirrelly." The Dun-in man smiled at that. Squirrelly, hiding nuts. Scampering away when a big dog came into the yard.

The land began to dip down, stretching towards a low plain. The Dun-in man knew the river of ice lay beyond. How frozen the river was remained to be seen. Toxicity played hell with water temps. He'd have to wait and see if there was a way across. It had been some weeks since he last saw the river. His heart warmed to it.

The fat man's name was Tony. And he was going towards the last northern colony. If it even remained. The Dun-in man had not seen the last holdfast in some years. It lay at the edge of a city, an old monastery off the main roads, buried deep in the barren forests. Back when the waters rose, and the toxic event happened, wreaking havoc in the cities, the monastery had been a good place to hold up, deep water resources, interior gardens of glass, tall walls to fortify, old technology that wasn't dependent on electricity.

As little as a decade ago, as the colony's formed, there had been trade and news between the old monastery and his own colony, which had bunkered down northwest of Boston, in the crotch of the mountains where the rain could be filtered through the old granite, and where the toxic air, too leaden, couldn't crest the mountains. His own colony had groves of fruit trees, their own glass gardens, and miles and miles of caves to hew shelter from. Those had been the boom years, though they hadn't known it. The monastery sent traders and the Dun-in man led hunting parties all the way across the river.

Back when Tony had been magistrate. When Tony had traction.

The fat man had a house, just near the second interior wall, and a small generator.

The Dun-in man knew this because as the toxic air finally began to penetrate the soil east of the colony, and filter into the water flowing west into the colony, and as more and more refugees flooded their walls, the generator had to be removed to the medical tents in the caves.

The Dun-in man had oversaw the operation

himself.

But the fat man had not cared, not really. In fact, he seemed almost patriotic about it.

"For the better good, no?" Tony had smiled at the Dun-in man, pulling on his peckish moustache, deliciously pointed and greased. "What I can do I will do." His smile suggested otherwise.

The Dun-in man knew people like that from his youth, as the waters had risen to flood Boston, forcing him and his family out of Brighton and into the western counties which were becoming angry pockets of poverty. And people like the fat man were there to welcome the poor, and then take all their money while smiling and shaking their hands and promising more, more, more. And did more ever come?

Not for the Dun-in man. Shortly after the waters took back Boston Harbor, and took back the park, and trickled into the neighborhoods, his father had left the western counties with the Dun-in man in tow, a little blond child by the name of Shawn, freshly ten, lanky and quick. They went back to Boston to plunder and pirate. His old man had some family property just inside the low-lying area, a place where they could hide away and store what they found. Government agencies, slowed by red-tape, doubt, and growing financial problems did not anticipate the rising waters. The Dun-in man looked back at this as foreshadowing. In a few years the toxic clouds that covered the east would set up a whole new emergency, and kill off what populations still scratched out a living in the flooded reeftown cities.

But back when he was Shawn and his father was

alive, and the stiltwalkers and skiff pirates had not yet formed full brigades, the city was open to explore, plunder, and wander. The National Guard left large gaps in their line so it was easy for Shawn and his dad to slip in, go to his great grandfather's little house and hold up. No one paid any attention. So little Shawn and his father fashioned ten foot stilts to carry down to the flooded downtown area and roam the high tide streets pillaging and looting. After his throat had been cut, his father built the skiff and the two of them paddled and foraged and gathered money and foodstuffs to take back to the families waiting in the camps. And they had done well, despite his throat, and despite the danger.

He should have stayed with the skiff pirates and stiltwalkers. Should have stayed and outlasted the toxic clouds. They bowled west and east and festooned above the mountains for a while before heading to the interior, or out to Europe over the sea. Now, some say, the east coast is the safest, the heavy toxins already purged, already cleansed by the earth. In his mind the Dun-in man could see them now, the skiffs, outfitted with plastic, even bone, cut metal hulls and platforms bolted, taped, and weaved together to skim the waters between the streets of the city, to cut over across the roofs of short buildings which had sunken into the weakened streets. The stiltwalkers, like water bugs moving in low tide, the men and women and children riding them leaning over to fish the salt brine for anything of use with their long eight foot hooks.

And in the city floods, at least there had been fish, those weird mussels that took to growing on the sides of the tall buildings as the waters continued to rise, rise, rise. How the moss men farmed them, popping them open and eating them while they were on stilts or on their skiffs, gulping the mucoid thing back into their throat.

The Dun-in man didn't think he could be a mossman, a building dweller. Moss men, because of how their skin and teeth took on a green taint. A city marsh punk, scraping together a home in the damp caves of an old office or apartment, throwing bolo wires at seabirds and spearing fish from low windows. Those buildings weren't all safe. He preferred the way the skiff pirates found places upland, just shy of the water, to live and gather.

It was one of them that took his voice, a big throated fellow with a machete made from roadside steel. He couldn't have been much younger than his father, and was already so dirty from living in the citymarsh that his face and hair had been matted with dirt, mud, feces, some muck seeping up from the sewers that made living in the city caves so dangerous.

"You were a fool to challenge him for that ax." His father had said to him as he bandaged his wound, pouring mercurochrome over the cut and pressing into his windpipe with his palm. "Foolish. You are lucky he did not strike so deep. You may be able to speak when it is healed. You were foolish."

The Dun-in man had wanted to say no, had wanted to explain that the ax had been found by him, lying under some three feet of water in a uptown firehouse. He had found it looking for hose to steal when the big fellow had come from behind.

"That's mine stilt-boy. All mine." The man had

growled.

The mossman was wet from the waist down, his hair greasy and unkempt, tied back with nylon cord. His beard wasn't long but thick, and the Dun-in man guessed his adversary had been in city since the water had risen over the sandbags. Had probably never left. He filled the air with a sharp sweet stink.

"I found it. I claim it." Shawn had said, his own blade already drawn.

"I don't honor no claiming rights," he had grunted.

The swinging blade caught him off guard and Shawn fell back against an old desk which had been overturned. His head cracked and his mind splintered into pain, but he got up. He moved. His own blade was longer, true. A bowie knife his father had found for him in one of the college dorms they had looted months back when they first came incity.

Steel clashed and sparks flew. Shawn edged forward, fear in his mouth like a wet copper penny. His thicker blade held back the mossman's homemade machete.

The mossman was stronger, but slower, enough so Shawn drew first blood, cutting the moss man deep on the upper arm.

"You little fuck." The man winced at his wound, and Shawn felt pride well up in him, which in the end cost him, for he did not leap fast enough, and could not beat back the man whose weight and extra muscle were enough to swing in so close and lay a cut across Shawn's throat.

Shawn gurgled, the blood coming faster, and

his head swooned, surely he was dying.

And that had been when his father had found them, just as the mossman was reeling back to finish the job.

His father didn't fire the pistol, instead he fired the flare and set the mossman's back and hair on fire, the flare burning deep into the mossman's skin, forcing the man out of the building, out into the air, screaming, the smell of roasted flesh, not unlike pig, filling the air of the uptown firehouse.

"What were you thinking?" His father asked, his fingers gingerly tending to him, loving him in a way that he would never know again. So long ago.

When the Dun-in man looked up the river lay below him, jagged and throated full of ice. The water flowed and careened over the floes that jammed up against each other. A piece of grey ice lay across a small bend. The falling snow had thinned, and the grey forest around him leaned and lay across each other.

He squinted in the light. The grey ice wasn't grey ice. It was metal. At least he thought so, a metal bridge. He shielded his eyes, an old habit, but it did not help. He would have to move closer.

It wasn't grey ice, but a large grey steel door torn from a truck. Tony probably found it at the edge of the river when he came up country. The bend in the river was no more than a few feet, hell, Tony could have jumped over, but then again the weather may have made Tony unsure. Tony was older than he, and out of shape. The Dun-in man stopped and sat down on the bank and went into his inner pockets for some jerky.

It burned his mouth as he chewed, and he reached back into his inner pockets for the pine broth canteen. He needed the vitamin C, and the broth would at least cool him, and coat his mouth, his throat too. While he was stopped, he filled his water skins and added the iodine and detoxifier. With luck he'd boil it too, if he could find firewood beyond the river. While he chewed, he rubbed his calves, thighs, and chest, keeping his blood circulating.

The sun began to sink low, mid-afternoon, and the Dun-in man would have a few more hours before he'd have to find shelter, somewhere he could build a fire and warm his bones. He reached into the other inner pocket and pulled out his old pipe and tobacco wrap. He was running low, and pinched off a fingernail sized bit of leaf and lit it. He removed his long rifle from his shoulder and checked the sights, checked the safety, and made sure the white rags he'd wrapped it in hadn't become wet in his travels. Satisfied he re-slung the weapon, stood, and put his things back inside the deer hide pockets. He balanced his feet upon the bank and walked over the panel of some lorry that had fallen off the road back when the world was still alive.

He slowed his pace. The snow came down in fat flakes, white and crystallized, and gleaming with the light of the fading sun. And the Dun-in man felt young once more, as if he were looking at a winter snow from before the rising waters, and from before the toxic wastes. The terrain went uphill, and the Dun-in man turned east, towards where the roads still lay in ruin. It took him another half-hour before his feet found the rising walls of the road to where the highway stretched out above the fields. The trees had thinned up along the road from the poor soil, and the way up was littered in thin fallen pines and silver oaks. The Dun-in man did not want to break his foot, or leg, so slowed his pace to an old man's crawl, making sure each step was sure. It took him the better part of an hour to move a few hundred yards, but once he was on the road, the way became easier.

If he stayed east he'd eventually hit the side roads that would take him to the last holdfast, but that would take time. The thought tempted him, the footing was sure, the vehicles long pulled over and scavenged by people long ago dead or moved out. Better to find shelter and then cut across the old way, the straight way, he thought.

So he walked, and soon came across an old rest stop. Under the snowfall the undergrowth, tangled weeds and briars, circled the building like a set of tentacles.

He stooped and shook the heavy snow from the dead vegetation. He couldn't tell how alive the briars had been, but he was sure this kind of growth was relatively new. Again the old hope rose up in him and he felt, what...happy? Lightened.

He unslung his rifle and bolted a round into the chamber. He loosened his bowie knife, and the bonds on his machete.

The front of the building was glass, and though it was cracked it was intact. From where he stood he could see nothing inside but trash and refuse, old maps spilled out onto the floor. Still, he listened, his old hunting habit, and walked past the front door to check the side. More growth, more briars, all relatively new. In the parking lot a few old cars and trucks lay covered in a foot of snow, barely recognizable from the landscape itself. Beyond, the old highway stretched on and on and on, white, winking and glistening in the falling light.

He saw no footprints but his own, and heard no sound but the lonely sound of his own body.

Turning back to the front door, he held his breath and pushed inside.

The first time he had ever gone into a deserted building had been after the waters had risen. He knew they had been abandoned, quite a different story from the later years after the toxins had spread, the living sick holding up wherever they could, to die, usually. Those that didn't die lived in pain and agony, and some of them even went on to make children, to make mutant babies born into the world hairless and white and blind.

The sickness which raged through the northern cities had moved on, and those that did not get the toxic sickness remained to fight over resources, of which there were few. And that's when people turned on each other. Those that didn't get sick seemed immune, or resistant, and became crueler. He half expected to find a family held up inside, a father, thin and angry, a mother still breast feeding her oldest child because there was simply no better way. But this wasn't the past and he didn't have to fight off a father and his son, and kill them both in front of the mother and the child. He didn't have to kill the mother first, and then the young boy, barely alive anyway, to make sure he slept safely that night. The inside was empty as a tomb.

He leaned back against the old counter and made sure he could see the road from where he lay. The dirty windows and the snow offered little view, but he felt better, more secure. He took off his pack and his wrap. He made a small torch of the yellowed paper on the ground, pressing the trash into the cylinder cage of wire attached to a long wooden handle. The yellowed paper made fast fuel and lit the old building up.

He slung his rifle and with one hand kept feeding the light, stuffing the old travel pamphlets and maps into the cage. He almost stumbled over a dead body, a skeleton. A man from the looks of it. His skull smashed in long ago. The clothes were dry rotted. The vending machines had all been looted, the glass broken across the floor. Smashed furniture lay about. There was enough paper and splintered furniture for a fire..

The ceiling of the main hall was high enough that the smoke wouldn't curl down and choke him, but the wood was so dry that the fire was smokeless, hot, and made hot coals for him to boil his water, and to brew some pine broth tea, and to make a weak soup from jerky and dried vegetables.

After he ate he took his torch and his small toolkit and tore at the guts of the vending machine, taking long copper wires from the controls. He could use them as ties, or handcuffs, or trade them at the colony to the quartermaster.

Sleep took him in long gulps, swallowed him and spat him out in the early dark. Something had stirred, but the Dun-in man could not tell if it were dream or real. He waited, still as a bone, his hand on the machete, but sleep took him again and he didn't wake up until the sun was high over the rest-stop.

He fixed a meager breakfast and packed his gear and headed west to cut a straight line to the holdfast. The snow had stopped and the world glittered back. A easy wind cut across his form. He pushed through the drifts and walked out under the sunlight.

The laughter took him out of memory.

The laughter made him freeze in his tracks.

Instinct dropped him to his knees and he lay flat against the earth. Ahead, in a clearing not a hundred yards away, stood three figures, most likely men, poking at a body on the ground. They laughed and held their machetes, and what looked like a spear, at the prone body.

Think, the Dun-in man thought. You are in the middle of a snowy brake. The woods offer no cover. You have made tracks. If they look they will discover you.

The largest of the figures threw back his hat and revealed himself to be a young man. He carried a pointed spear forged from scrap metal and a long handle of some kind. The figures wore a motley get up of white patchwork clothing. They looked thin, hungry, desperate. The man on the ground was Tony, the fat man.

He had been crying, and was crying, and would continue to cry. A long rope had been tied to his neck and it looked like the group had been leading him. Possibly the holdfast. The old monastery was close.

The largest figure shouted orders, his accent rough, his voice hoarse. The three pulled the fat man up, and pushed through the snow. As they walked slowly over the terrain, a county road offshoot from the old highway, the Dun-in man could see that they had no rifles, no firearms, save for what may have been hidden under their wraps. But by the way they moved, he didn't think they were heavily armed.

He waited till they were out of binocular range before he followed, taking care not to rattle the old dead trees. Any blur of movement could alert them to his presence, and he needed to catch them unawares.

His rifle, he kept loaded, safety on, in his hands as he trudged just away from the county road, near the line of deadfall. He could, at any time, fall into the ground and vanish from sight.

Following them for two hours, he closed the distance, and began to see signs of the last holdfast nearby, the old street signs marking the distance, an exit sign long ago stripped from a pole, the remnants of a few small tourists traps. When night came he found the back of an old convenience store and wedged his way inside. Through his binoculars he could see the orange glow of their fire, some two hundred yards under an overpass. They seemed to pay him no mind, and grew comfortable with his distance from them the more he watched the fire; he saw that they had not doubled back, even for firewood.

The plan was to overtake them in the morning, outpace them, and come around before they reached the holdfast and take the fat man from them. The snow might give his tracks away, but he hoped to take them before they discovered him. The men might give him news of the holdfast, of whom and what still lived there, but would likely choose death before disclosing any secret to an outsider, especially one with a rifle.

But he didn't sleep. Without a roaring fire the shelter drafted and blew and breezed and made his sleep rattle with cough.

Dreams troubled him, too, a tight series of dreams that began with his father and ended with his mother. The strange woman Terry, back in the colony, sometimes spoke to men and women about their dreams. She was of the snake and spoke two voices, one of man, and one of woman, and the Dun-in mad had been to shy to approach her. He was afraid of what she would say. She translated dreams and omens for the poor minded. If he lived he would consult her.

In one his teeth had come out in his hands, and in another he was swallowed by a wave of dirt. In them, he was small, feverish. Tiny as a bean.

In the early dark he abandoned his shelter and traveled northeast of the group. He hiked up the hill into the rocky purchases out of their sight line, though he might be spotted by other colonists, from behind. If there were any. The unknown lay in stomach like rich food, it made him slightly sick.

As he came up on the old colonies' walls of stone, and his senses sharpened. He kept his big knife loose in its sheath. He expected a fire of sorts, but found none. In the dark he found the watchtower, the old belltower, unmanned.

He had walked up to the old monastery's outer wall without realizing it. What unsettled him was that no one had noticed.

It was his nose that told him part of the story.

He found a cupola that should have been the guardhouse, but it was bare. A bit of rag and wet hay on the floor. No firewood. No canned goods, no trash. Nothing. It smelled fresh. Clean almost.

No one had lived there for some weeks, perhaps months. Whether from cold or from toxic winds he did not know. The monastery had not, or could not man the wall.

He rested long enough to drink pine broth and eat jerky. He shouldered his rifle and drew his machete. The bowie he kept under his wrappings.

There were two more cupolas before the stone walkway arched up to the bell tower. The sun had not broken; he could see it building the east, a pink quickening.

The tower he found empty. Clean.

They're all dead, he thought. Dead, or dying.

Then who are those men with the fat man?

The last. the last of them.

He examined the lock, the hinges of the bell tower door, hanging to the side. It had been ripped off. Gouges in the wood.

It started to snow.

At least your tracks will be covered. That's some comfort.

He was to bring Tony back for punishment.

That was his objective.

He was now sure Tony was being led here for food.

He could simply wait for them, and pick them off. Assuming there was no one else living here.

Better to be sure.

The stairs out of the tower smelled of stale death, and he drew his knife and carefully edged his way down.

But it was as he thought. No sign of life other than a few ripped pieces of stained cloth. A few old broken bottles, crushed by boots coming or going.

He moved beyond the tower and checked the other side of the wall and found equally empty rooms. The sun rose and illuminated the road towards the monastery. A perfect path of white. A mile away, smoke from a campfire.

At the bottom of the courtyard in a little exposed opening where the hill dipped away, he spied three doorways that descended into the stone. Under the hill, out of sight and in the darkness. Offices and classrooms where the old monks would lecture and read. There were more chambers underground, the wells and the storehouses. If he were to find anyone alive they'd be deep under the earth, deep in a natural crotch in the hills.

The Dun-in man turned a corner and slipped into the deep dark narrow corridor that led underground.

The smell stopped him in his tracks.

Meat. Roasted meat. And blood. And something sickly sweet underneath it all.

They've turned cannibal.

They did want to eat Tony.

They'd be easy targets if they had been too long without other nutrition. If. That was always the case. If they had nothing else to eat but each other then they'd be vulnerable. But his mother always warned him to not wish his life away.

The descent took him through cluttered rooms, dark and unlit, though at one time there had been candles, he could tell from the dark streaks up the wall.

At one time the colony had been over a hundred strong. How many people lived here now he could not say, but the early indications were that most of them were dead. There were only ghosts here.

He found the trussing room towards the back hall where the structure branched out. One of the larger rooms stank of blood. Candles, no bigger than his knuckle, were jammed into the candlesticks that once lit mass. Their orange yellow color told him all he needed to know, liver fat. In a pinch they could be used as food with a little flour, or meal. But he did not take them, though he knew plenty of outlay scouts who used fat candles. Whether they used human or animal fat he did not know. He did take a coil of rope, gory as it was, from the corner where they were looped. This would be where they would take Tony to string him up and dress him. There were no signs of bones, but in the adjacent room he found a long display of skulls that numbered four and sixty.

It was then he heard the first human voice in

the monastery, and drew his rifle to shoulder. Caution steeled him and he stepped towards the sound down the hall. A rail thin woman muttered to herself as she handled a large hunk of meat, a thigh by the looks of it. Whom she muttered to he did not know, for there was no one else but she kept looking up at a portrait on the wall, the back of her neck craning as she looked to it. She did not see the Dun-in man until she turned to fetch her butcher's blade.

She blinked twice, and shrieked.

He hesitated, and in that second of pause she threw the blade at him, and it came at him handle over handle and struck the barrel of his rifle and caused him to misfire.

He cursed her and dashed towards her. She ran away towards a counter running along the edge of the room. He saw the dull gleam of more blades.

They met, and she screamed and fell bone against bone, and with a quick turn he broke her neck. The shrieking stopped. But not for long.

Someone echoed back a long moan. Short piercing cries followed.

That's not the sound of humanity, he thought, that's the sound of a world dying.

What followed was a thundering of feet, light feet, but feet that made noise all the same and he heard them come up the hallway that led below the quarters where the monks had once made beer and the survivors now lived in tight clutches like lice.

He did not fire, he did not have the bullets to do so, and fled, and behind him came two dozen small women and children, but wilden, emboldened, hungry, lean from eating nothing but human flesh and living in the dark since the spring.

The stench gagged him and his reptilian brain urged him to run faster. The smell of rotten flesh and curdled blood rolled out before their ragged bodies.

When he ran out of the lower levels and back into the courtyard, the sun had crested the dead trees and there was no more smoke in the sky. Those he had tracked were on their way, and may even be already bearing down on him.

A few of the children beared down on him, and he would have to run faster or fight. And as he came out from under the arches that once wove down the hillsides to the city, he saw the party, and fat Tony being pulled behind, his face a red chugging gasping hole.

The first shot took him by surprise but missed him entirely, and he tripped and fell over, and the little beasts behind him piled on him, biting, scratching, clawing.

He pushed his fingers through the first child's eyes until it was dead and unclamped from his thigh and he used it to bludgeon the next small thing that had decided to claw for his face. He fought them back until he got his machete loose and began to chop at them. That scared them enough to hold back, and the Dun-in man stood bleeding, surrounded. The men he had trailed now formed the centerpiece of their attack. The smallest of them held up a short rifle, a .22, perhaps, and was aiming it at him. The big one dropped the rope dragging Tony and prepared to charge.

The young ones growled and hissed and spoke memes and phonemes, their language as spare as their diet. He would not be able to use his rifle, but if he could manage it, could get to his pistol.

The party regarded him with danger, and for the first time he saw that they were older children, no older than eighteen, maybe nineteen, but worn thin and old.

This is when a voice would be helpful, but after listening to them he didn't think it mattered. These people had been alone for a long time. He would have to shoot his way out.

His mind slipped into a relaxed state. His gun hand went to his pistol at his back, and the spare hand went to the ammo belt, ready to reload. The Dun-in man shot the lead boy in the forehead, the one with a rifle and when he fell back his rifle went off, sending the circle of foes into a panicked frenzy.

One of the children grabbed his spare hand and bit him on the wrist. For that, the child received a pistol butt in the forehead. It made a sickening crunch where it struck and the wild child fell off. He shot at the spear bearers, but not before a small dirty girl took a knife to Tony and cut him across the chest. Tony screamed and grasped at his wound, the cut fur and lining of his clothes tumbling out out like fresh snow.

Maybe he wasn't hurt too bad, the Dun-in man thought, and killed the last armed kid with a shot that took out his eye.

The wild boys scattered, hooting and crying into the dark. A spear missed him and bounced away in the snow. The Dun-in man shot a hole in the young man's cheek, dropping him.

And the Dun-in man did not wait and grabbed Tony by the shoulder and led him away, back the way he came.

"My God, my God. They were going to eat me." Tony cried and blubbered.

They ran as fast as they could down the road. Behind them the wild children and women leaped about like animals. One of them had picked up the rifle.

The Dun-in man pushed Tony ahead, dropping to a knee and bringing his own long rifle to bear. Through the scope he aimed for the skull and squeezed off a single shot that dropped the child in the snow.

They would follow.

Fat Tony ran as far as he could, and when they came to the place where Tony and his captors had spent the night, they paused.

Tony started to ask lots of questions until he remembered to whom he spoke to and dropped it.

"I forgot. Your voice." Tony said. "I'm sorry."

The Dun-in man nodded and shrugged.

Behind them the wild ones would be already be dragging their dead to butcher.

The knife had cut through the lining of his jacket and scratched his chest, but it was superficial wound and the Dun-in man bound it before tending to his own cuts and scrapes and bites. They shared pine broth and moved on.

He communicated to Tony by gesture and mime.

"I only wanted to see if someplace else was better," Tony stammered. "We hadn't heard from them in so long."

It was never better. At least in the north. Perhaps things improved in the south, but he did not think so. Not since the waters had risen had things looked so bleak. But even after the waters had risen, things had gotten better, if only for a while.

They walked through the day and into sunset. They camped at the rest stop and ate all of the Dun-in man's provisions except for the pine broth in the water skins. The next day they made it back to the colony, exhausted, thinner, and famished.

Karl met them at the gates, a wicked smile on his lips. He looked wolfish in his winter skins, and the Dun-in man smiled at him; he greeted him with a hearty handshake.

"Take Tony back," he told his two guards, "Set up dinner." He turned to the Dun-in man and clapped him on the shoulder. "I bet you need your rest. We have much to discuss and I want you to write down everything you remember. Before it gets lost in one of your whisky binges. And I do have a good bottle set aside for you. One of the last of the real whiskys, none of Al's homemade shit."

The Dun-in man smiled, his bones hurt. His fingers hurt. Where he had been bitten hurt. He rubbed his hands together and watched the back of Tony's head vanish behind the wide canvas tents that were set up just inside the palisade walls. The place smelled of woodsmoke and roasting pine nuts. Someone sang a song, the chorus echoed up and out, "Hotel California."

The singing made him shudder, because he knew what was coming for them all. He knew it before he long set out to bring back the fat man. The truth of it lay in his gut. He knew it like a stone in the road, something that was eventual and truthful and dumb.

He didn't know he knew it, but when it came to him at dinner, later that night, he accepted it. After he had bathed and warmed his body with fresh clothes and a whiskey, they brought him the dish of turnips and a cut of meat which was the tender flesh of fat Tony's neck. He was not surprised, nor shocked, only disappointed that once again he had thought he was fighting on the winning side, when like everything else in life there was no winning side. When the game was played long enough everyone lost. The Dun-in man knew then his time with the colony was at the end, but he did not let it show in his face. He picked up his fork and put it to his plate. He even smiled when the first bite melted in his mouth.

.·.

Stephen Scott Whitaker is a member of National Book Critics Circle, and the literary review editor for The Broadkill Review. His poetry, fiction, and essays have appeared in dozens of publications. His previous chapbooks include the steampunk inspired The Black Narrows, the award winning Field Recordings, The Barleyhouse Letters, and All My Rowdy Friends. Whitaker teaches theater, literature and psychology in rural Maryland. He lives on the Eastern Shore of Virginia with his family.